Specky
Magee

Here I am as an 11-year-old in Kyabram, Victoria. I've just been awarded a medal for champion swimmer at my primary school, St Augustine's. It was one of the most memorable days of my school life. That, and when I took the greatest mark over Garry Lyon!

Even back then, Garry was a footy star. Every boy in our school knew that he was destined for football greatness. During our lunchtimes, when we weren't playing British Bulldog or Releaso (hard-hitting running games popular with schoolboys in the 1970s and '80s), Grades Five and Six would sweat it out in major footy battles on the school oval.

One lunchtime I was positioned to play on Garry (he was in Grade Six, I was in Grade Five). The ball made its way toward us and I knew that I had nothing to lose being up against such a champion. So like the Six Million Dollar Man (my favourite TV hero at the time), I took the greatest leap of my life. I flew metres above Garry's shoulders, amazingly grabbed and held onto the ball with one hand. Everyone looked on in complete shock, especially Garry. No one had ever taken a successful mark — let alone a sensational 'specky' — from him before. For that split moment in time I was a legend!

Yep, those were the days. What? You don't believe me? Okay, maybe it didn't happen *exactly* like that. Maybe Garry was standing nearby and I took the mark over someone who looked like him ... or, maybe it was just a chest-mark kicked to me *by* Garry. Okay, okay, my memory might be a little hazy, but Garry and I *were* schoolmates, and, well ... I did win that swimming medal!

Happy reading!

Felice

Well, if Felice is going to brag about his swimming medals, I thought it only fair that I dig out a photo of one of my most prized possessions — my first Victorian U/15 Schoolboys' football jumper. I would have been all of (a very lean) 14 years of age at the time, and it involved flying to Adelaide to play footy against all the other States and Territories. It was truly the highlight of my life, with the added bonus of missing a few days of school back at St Augustine's in Kyabram. Heaven!

And as for Felice and that 'mark'! It is obvious why Felice has become such a successful children's author — he has a very strong imagination, which he has used to write some terrific stories. A bit like the one he dreamed up about taking a mark over me.

We used to love it when Felice joined in for kick-to-kick at lunchtime, as he was the best player to practice taking 'speckies' on. I will concede that he was a very good swimmer and gained fame throughout our school for that fact.

Hope you enjoy the book. I think there's a little bit of Specky, and his family, in all of us.

Garry

The life and times of an aspiring
footy champion . . .

Specky
Magee

FELICE ARENA

AND

GARRY LYON

Angus&Robertson
An imprint of HarperCollins*Publishers*

Angus&Robertson

An imprint of HarperCollins*Publishers*, Australia

First published in Australia in 2002
Reprinted in 2002 (nine times), 2003 (five times)
by HarperCollins*Publishers* Pty Limited
ABN 36 009 913 517
A member of the HarperCollins*Publishers* (Australia) Pty Limited Group
www.harpercollins.com.au

HarperCollins*Publishers*

25 Ryde Road, Pymble, Sydney NSW 2073, Australia
31 View Road, Glenfield, Auckland 10, New Zealand
77–85 Fulham Palace Road, London W6 8JB, United Kingdom
2 Bloor Street East, 20th floor, Toronto, Ontario M4W 1A8, Canada
10 East 53rd Street, New York NY 10022, USA

National Library of Australia Cataloguing-in-publication data:

Arena, Felice.
    Specky Magee.
    For children aged 10–13 years.
    ISBN 0 207 19829 2.
    1. Australian football – Juvenile fiction.
    2. Adopted children – Juvenile fiction.
    3. Family – Juvenile fiction.
    I. Lyon, Garry. II. Title.
A823.3.

Cover image: Getty Images
Author photos courtesy of Felice Arena and Garry Lyon
Designed by Lore Foye, HarperCollins Design Studio
Printed and bound in Australia by Griffin Press on 80gsm Econoprint

18 17 16 15   03 04 05 06

1

SATURDAY PLAY

'Come on, get the ball down here,' mumbled Specky under his breath.

Specky and his team-mates had to play the best footy ever, especially if they were to have any chance of winning today's competition. He guessed there were about two minutes of the game left to go, and the opposition were ahead by just five points.

Hugging the boundary line of Specky's school oval were parents, teachers and other onlookers. They screamed and cheered their support. They all knew the importance of this particular game. Specky and his team, the Booyong High Lions, were playing the top team on the ladder, the Beacon Hill Falcons. The Lions were placed second to the Falcons only by percentage — a win today definitely meant reversed positions.

'Stop mucking about! Stop hand-balling! Kick the ball long! Long!' shouted Specky's team coach, Mr Pappas. His entire face turned a bright beetroot colour as he let out his frustration. He was a proud, fair and emotional coach who worshipped the great game of Aussie Rules — and for that reason alone, everyone loved him. Mr Pappas desperately hoped his team could quickly get the ball over to Specky, because for the past four games in a row, Specky had proven that he was the star player. He had single-handedly kicked over seven goals in each game he played, and was the best full-forward in their local schools league.

Specky frantically shuffled back and forth in the goal square, trying desperately to put some space between himself and the opposition's full-back. But he wasn't having much success. The determined, stocky player stuck to him like glue. Specky tried his best to ignore his opponent's off-putting remarks.

'I think you'll look good on crutches, you loser! You'd better hope the ball doesn't come this way, or you're dead meat!' he snarled, while nudging and jabbing his elbow into Specky's ribs.

 Specky knew, from spending hours and hours watching and listening to his heroes, players such as Matthew Lloyd and Nathan Buckley, about the need to stay focused on what was happening on the field and not to get 'sucked in' by his opponent. Matthew Lloyd always said to look upon the extra attention as a compliment, a sign that you were playing well and had the opposition worried. That is how he had decided to cope with taggers.

Specky couldn't help thinking that his opponent's huffing and puffing was like the sound of some kind of wild bush pig, about to make a sudden ferocious charge.

Yeah, right, we'll see who the loser is, thought Specky. He wasn't going to let the guy intimidate him.

Specky could see that the action of the game was focused around the centre of the ground. It was hard for him to pinpoint who exactly had the ball. There was a lot of scrappy tackling going on, which resulted in numerous stop and start ball-ups by the umpire.

Then, out of nowhere, Specky spotted Josh Roberts — known to his mates as 'Robbo' — taking clean possession of the ball. He was one of Specky's best friends, and the team's ruckman — he was a tall lanky boy who towered above everyone else. Looking at him, you wouldn't think he was only in Year Seven. He looked more as if he belonged in Year Nine.

'Robbo! Robbo!' shouted Specky's team-mates.

Robbo looked up-field for his forward-line players. He had a clear break from the opposition. Specky suddenly sensed that the ball was finally heading his way. He shot another quick glance at the scoreboard — time was running out.

Please don't sound the siren, not yet, he wished.

He could hear Robbo's proud dad, who was standing beside Coach Pappas, shouting out encouraging words to his son. 'That's it, Josh, all the way, boy!'

Specky couldn't help but wonder how great it must be to get that sort of encouragement. He wished his own father was in the crowd supporting him.

'Over here, I'm free!'

It was Danny Castelino, another one of Specky's close friends, and Booyong High's number one rover. While Robbo was one of the tallest kids in Specky's school, Danny was definitely one of the shortest. He looked as if he should have been back in primary school — but that didn't stop him being one of the toughest and most determined players on the team. No one could stop him. He was as fit as a greyhound, and could run nonstop for an entire game.

Robbo acknowledged Danny by spearing the ball directly into his chest. It was a safe mark, but Danny didn't have the luxury of taking his time. He charged off towards the forward pocket area.

The pass was perfect, travelling no higher than a metre off the ground, covering the distance to Danny in a split second, not giving his opponent a chance to punch the ball away.

Like Robbo, Danny's father was also cheering for him on the sideline. Again, Specky took note of this, and strangely enough, so did the full-back.

'Is that his dad? My dad's over there. Where's yours?' he asked casually, still trying to bump and push Specky off his feet.

'He's not here, he's not into footy,' Specky replied in a somewhat disappointed tone.

In the meantime, Danny was making a run for it. He took one bounce, then another, and another. The opposition was closing in on him. One boy in particular was dashing towards him from the wing. Totally unaware of the boy's speedy oncoming presence, Danny continued to baulk and weave past another two players. It was an exciting passage of play by Danny, but very risky at the same time.

Danny knew that there was a fine line between being the hero or villain in a team. He had, on occasions, tried to do too much with the football, lost possession in the process, and cost his team the match. But he had also been the hero, capable of inspiring solo runs that eventually led to match winning goals. Specky hoped that this was one of those times.

Specky could see his friend clearly now. He timed his lead to sprint away from the full-back. 'Danny!' he shouted after him.

14

The boy chasing Danny was only millimetres away from grabbing him and throwing him to the ground. Coach Pappas was beginning to lose his voice from screaming at the top of his lungs.

'Get rid of it! Look out, he's behind you!' he croaked.

But it was too late. The boy from Beacon Hill had successfully taken a firm grip of Danny's jumper. Under pressure, Danny did his best to get rid of the ball — he had been brutally stopped dead in his tracks. With no time to think, he dropped the football onto his right foot and booted it with all his might.

Miraculously, the unbalanced kick had some power behind it. A gust of wind aided it high into the sky, and as if it was captured in slow-motion, the ball floated towards the goal square, directly above Specky. It was a rainmaker of a kick. So much so that the players had difficulty spotting it in the blinding glare of the sun — but not Specky.

He hadn't for a moment taken his eye off the ball. The full-back shoved himself in front of Specky, getting ready to punch the ball away. Specky took a step back, fully aware that the ball had now begun its rapid descent towards the ground. With one giant leap, he was suddenly airborne. He propped his right knee securely between the shoulder blades of his pig-like opponent and catapulted his entire stretched-out body high above the players around him. Specky's opponents watched, and their jaws dropped in admiration, stunned by his amazing display. Even Specky's team-mates, who had seen such aerial magic many times before, looked on with admiration. They were proud to witness their full-forward's gift in taking high-flying marks. True to his nickname, Specky had certainly taken a **spec**tacular 'specky'!

 For Specky there was no other feeling quite like taking a big grab. He had a natural gift for being able to maintain perfect balance while perched on an opponent's shoulders. With arms outstretched, fingers well spread and eyes fixed on the ball, he was never going to drop it. The other impressive part of Specky's aerial antics was his catlike ability to always land on his feet, unlike other players who, in their attempt to outdo him, would land awkwardly, injuring a shoulder, or twisting an ankle. Specky practised his high

*marking by kicking the ball onto the roof of
his house, and then timing his run to jump at
exactly the split second the ball came
bouncing down off the tiles and spilling over
the guttering. It improved his marking
dramatically, but got him into lots of trouble
with his dad for breaking the odd tile here
and there. And it annoyed his sister, Alice,
who claimed that she couldn't hear whoever
it was she was talking to on the phone with
his football constantly banging on the roof.*

With a confident grip on the ball, the mark
was taken directly in front of the big sticks.
Specky landed on the ground with a thud and
grinned to himself as he heard the umpire's
whistle sound the end of the game. Specky was
allowed to take his kick for goal. If he missed,
his team would lose. He took a deep breath and
lined up his kick.

2

FOOTY BLOOD

'Chewy on ya boot ... woo, woo, ya gonna miss!' The full-back and his team-mates waved their arms, teased, and did whatever they could to distract Specky. But Specky ignored them all. Determined not to get flustered, he even blocked out the excited screams of the coach and his team-mates' parents. There was no way he was going to miss this goal. Specky was 15 metres directly in front. It would be a simple straight kick.

But just as he was about to connect his boot to the ball, the full-back player shouted out, 'Too bad your dad can't see this, huh?'

Specky's concentration was instantly broken. The full-back's comment ran over and over in Specky's mind as he executed the kick. The ball made contact with the side of his boot and veered in a wobbly, sharp-right direction — away from the goals. Specky had missed! The unexpected 'shocker' resulted in scoring only a measly single behind. It was the worst kick of Specky's life. He had lost the game for his team — he couldn't believe it. Nor could his team-mates, who stood there stunned as the opposite side celebrated their victory. Specky was so embarrassed. He couldn't bear to look at his team as they sadly dawdled back to the changing rooms.

'I'm sorry, Coach, I didn't mean ...' Before Specky had a chance to apologise, Coach Pappas stopped him.

'Don't worry about it, kid, even AFL champions can have their bad luck moments. That's what makes footy so great — it's always so unpredictable. So let it go. You played a great game. In fact, I'm happy with everyone's game today.'

Specky was slightly comforted by his coach's sympathetic compliment, but he still couldn't help feeling disappointed in himself, and sorry for his team.

'See ya, Speck. Have a good weekend. Carn the Pies!' shouted Danny Castelino.

Danny and his dad, and all of Specky's other team-mates, were leaving to get on with the rest of the weekend. Danny was a die-hard Collingwood supporter, and most Saturdays after the game he and his family would go and barrack for their beloved black-and-white team. They were season members.

'You mean, "Go Swans!"' shouted Robbo, an avid Sydney supporter whose family had moved from there to Melbourne a few years ago.

'Did you want a lift home?' asked Robbo's father. Robbo's family lived only two streets away from Specky's house.

'No thanks, Mr Roberts. Dad shouldn't be too much longer,' said Specky.

But Specky may have spoken too soon. He watched everyone leave, until he was the only one left, waiting patiently for his father to pick him up. The time ticked by — ten, twenty, thirty minutes passed and still no sign of his dad. Specky decided to read a newspaper that one of the dads had given him. He naturally turned to the sporting pages first and read up on the AFL weekend games. But a particular article caught his eye. He slowly read it. It was all about some university research which

20

speculated that having a talent for playing football could be genetically passed on from one generation to the next. Specky reread part of the article:

Football blood. How deep does it run? If your father and his father before him were footy champions, then it's likely that you are destined to be a champion yourself — either at school, the local club or at a professional level. Look at the great champion families in AFL: the Hudsons, the Lloyds, the Silvagnis, the Fletchers, the Whitnalls, the Davises ...

Huh? thought Specky. His mind was racing. He thought about his own dad and himself. They were total opposites. His father wasn't into sport, especially football. He hadn't even played it as a kid at school. He absolutely hated footy.

'Football runs this city and state — it's on most nights of the week nowadays. There's footy TV shows on network and cable, you can't get away from it!' his dad would often whine.

In fact it was no surprise that when Specky expressed his interest in playing the game several years ago by wanting to be a part of Auskick, his dad had forbidden it. 'Football's a barbaric sport! I'm not allowing my child to get hurt on purpose! What about if I arrange pottery lessons or we could play chess instead?' he once said. But Specky had persisted. He pleaded with his dad for weeks on end, until eventually it paid off. He was finally permitted to play. Since then, there had been many times when Specky privately yearned for his father to just join him in the backyard for a friendly kick-to-kick game, or come and watch him play for his school. Even his team-mates' parents thought it was kind of sad that Specky's dad hadn't made any effort to support his son — especially since he was one of the team's best players.

Specky knew his father loved him, but he was never going to share Specky's enthusiasm for football. Specky was finding it increasingly difficult to get used to the fact that his father was a non-footy dad. Even his mother and his older sister couldn't care less about the game. Not once did his family get excited about things like the Brownlow Medal or that special 'one day' in September.

Specky glanced down at the newspaper article again. He wondered if he had any footy-blood in him at all. If he did, it certainly wasn't from his mum or dad, he thought.

One hour later, Specky's father finally turned up. Specky moped over to the car and got into the front passenger seat.

'I'm sorry I'm late, son. I have to blame work again.' Specky's father was the owner of an art gallery. 'I was stuck at the airport waiting for this incredibly talented Peruvian artist to fly in, and his plane was late. So, how did my front-forward man play?'

'*Full-forward*, Dad, not front-forward!' Specky sighed and gloomily dropped his head against the car window.

3

FOOTYHEAD

As soon as Specky got home he ran upstairs to the study, plonked himself in front of the computer and began surfing the Internet. He checked out all his favourite football websites, which he loved to do.

'Hey, squirt, don't be too long. I wanna check something out.' It was Specky's older sister, Alice, barging in. She was 14, and seemed to love bossing Specky around.

'Well, you'll have to wait. I've just got online,' replied Specky. He wasn't in any mood to argue with his sister after the day he'd had.

Alice leaned over his shoulder to take a closer look at the computer screen. 'Arggh! Always footy. There's more on the Internet than *footy*, you know,' she scoffed, then stormed out of the room.

Specky frowned. 'Well, not for me there isn't . . .' he mumbled to himself.

Once online, Specky joined a football chat room and was instantly messaged by someone called *CHRISkicks*. Specky's screen name was *FOOTYHEAD*. Someone else in cyberspace had already taken the screen name of 'Specky'.

CHRISkicks: Hi. Who do you think is going to win the game between the Crows and the Kangaroos today?

FOOTYHEAD: The Kangaroos. How old are you?

CHRISkicks: I'm 12 and that's the truth, I swear. I know people lie heaps in these chat rooms.

FOOTYHEAD: Yeah, I know. There's a few creeps out there. I'm 12, too.

CHRISkicks: So who do you barrack for? I barrack for Carlton. Come on the mighty Blues!

FOOTYHEAD: Is that where you live, in Carlton?

CHRISkicks: Yes. Do you live in Melbourne or somewhere else in Australia?

FOOTYHEAD: Yeah, I live in Melbourne, in Camberwell.

CHRISkicks: So, you must barrack for Hawthorn then? Since you live near there.

FOOTYHEAD: No, I don't.

CHRISkicks: Then who do you follow?

FOOTYHEAD: Well, I don't barrack for one team exactly. I barrack for five teams!

CHRISkicks: You what? That's crazy! How can you barrack for five teams?

It was true. As long as Specky could remember, he was unable to support just *one* AFL team. His friends, especially Robbo and Danny, used to affectionately tease him about it. They originally thought it was a cop-out, and pressured him for a long time to make up his mind and choose only one team. But Specky couldn't. He was an avid fan of the actual game rather than any specific team. So he decided to support a group of teams that he felt he had some sort of personal connection with. They were Essendon, West Coast Eagles, Brisbane Lions, Collingwood and Sydney. Essendon, because if he wasn't going to grow up to be a professional footy player, he would pursue a career as a fighter-bomber pilot. West Coast Eagles, because his grandfather lives in Perth, and he considers him to be pretty cool. Brisbane Lions because his school team are the Lions. And finally, Sydney because Robbo barracks for them; and Collingwood because of Danny.

CHRISkicks: So what happens if two of your teams get in the Grand Final. Who do you go for then?

FOOTYHEAD: I flip a coin to decide.

CHRISkicks: That's SO weird!

'Simon! I need your help please!' It was Specky's mother calling for him. She always called Specky by his real name, Simon. Specky's family members were the only ones to call him Simon. Everyone else, including

Specky's teachers, called him Specky — which he preferred.

Specky said a hurried goodbye to his new online friend and logged off to join his mother. She was cleaning out her wardrobe.

'Honey, I want you to take these boxes to the spare room. I'm making some more space here for my clothes. Thanks,' she said.

Specky obliged. Most of the heavy boxes were filled with general family memorabilia. While stacking the boxes away, Specky's curiosity got the better of him, and he casually started to sift through them. He was especially interested in one box that was piled to the top with loose photographs.

Specky chuckled to himself as he flipped through the images. In particular, a photo taken a year ago, showing Robbo, Danny and himself with birthday cake smeared across their faces. Specky remembered they'd had a huge food fight. It had been so cool.

Specky continued to sift through the photos until he stumbled onto something that caught his attention, exactly the same way the 'Footy-blood' newspaper article had done earlier in the day. But this time he wasn't smiling. It was an old photograph of him when he was about two years old. Specky knew it was him, but he'd never seen any photos like this one! What made this picture stand out from the rest was how Specky was dressed. He was decked out from head to toe entirely in football clothing — Geelong Cats attire, to be exact. Specky was wearing a Geelong Cats beanie, scarf, jumper, and even baby football boots.

This is so weird, thought Specky. He wondered why his mum and dad had dressed him up in footy gear if they hated the game so much. And why Geelong? They didn't even know anyone from Geelong.

Specky was totally baffled, but he was determined to find out the answers ...

4

PHOTO BLUES

Specky continued to stare at the photograph. He flipped it over, only to discover that there was something written on the back in pen. It read:

Simon, 18 months old.
Future footy champ and Cats supporter.

But I don't barrack for Geelong, thought Specky.

He examined the handwriting. It didn't look like his mum or dad's. He wondered who could possibly have written it.

Just then, Specky's mum barged into the room. He hurriedly shoved the photograph into his back pocket.

'I thought you were helping me!' said Specky's mother. She noticed the box filled with the family snapshots, and smiled. 'Oh, that's what you're up to. You're having a nostalgic moment, are you?'

Specky looked up at her blankly. He was considering whether or not to ask his mother straight out about the strange photograph. But he didn't know what to say, so he quizzed her with some lead-up questions instead, just like a TV lawyer would.

'Mum, do we have any relatives or friends in Geelong?'

'No. Why?'

'Just wondering. Do you or Dad have any friends who barrack for Geelong?'

'You mean the football team?'

Specky nodded.

'No, we don't. You know we don't. What's all this about?'

'Um, nothing.' Specky knew he would have to be more specific. 'When I was a baby, how did you dress me?'

Specky's mother had a confused expression on her face. 'What do you mean, how did I dress you?'

'Did you ever dress me up in, you know, like funny costumes or anything?' Specky felt he was closing in on his mum. Just as he had seen on TV so many times before. The lawyer would

31

surprisingly swoop down on the witness and put them on the spot, with nowhere else to go. His mum would have no other choice but to tell the truth.

'Never. I never put you in tacky costumes!' exclaimed Specky's mum.

'Well, what about AFL football clothes — scarfs, beanies, boots, all that sort of stuff?'

'Definitely not! Is this all about you wanting to get football clothes? Because you can if you want, but out of your own pocket money.'

Specky reached into his pocket. It was time to swoop. 'No, it's got nothing to do with that.' He pulled out the photograph and shoved it under his mother's nose. 'It's got to do with this. If you and Dad are against footy so much, then why did you dress me up like this? Can you remember when it was taken? And who wrote on the back of it?'

Specky's mother took a closer look at the picture, then flipped it over and read the inscription. Specky grinned to himself until he saw his mother suddenly turn pale and serious. Her voice began to quiver as she stumbled to give him an explanation.

'Um, um, maybe the babysitter dressed you up or something, I can't remember.'

Specky didn't believe her. His mother quickly changed the subject. 'Are you going to help me or not? I can't stand here and chat all day!' she snapped, then stormed out of the room.

Specky was more confused than ever now, and completely shocked by his mother's reaction.

She was obviously hiding something very important from him. But what? he wondered. Specky needed desperately to get some air and to talk this over with a friend. So he decided to head over to Robbo's house to get his opinion.

'Hey, I'm glad you're here!' shouted Robbo. Robbo was heading out the front door of his house just as Specky was coming through the front gate.

'Why?' asked Specky.

'You can help me try to find a birthday present for my dad. I'm just heading down to the shops.'

So Robbo and Specky made their way to the local shopping centre.

As they browsed through the sports store, Specky showed Robbo the unusual photograph, and filled him in on his mother's strange reaction to it.

'Don't tell me you barrack for the Cats now!' said Robbo.

'No, well, I'm not sure. Look, don't you think it's weird?'

Specky was a little annoyed that Robbo hadn't fully understood his concern.

'I s'pose so,' he answered. 'Maybe your mum was right, and it was the babysitter or something. You know, Geelong's not a bad team. Maybe you should go for them.'

Specky shook his head and rolled his eyes. Robbo just wasn't getting it. Instead, he changed the subject and continued to help his friend search for a gift.

5

COULD BE?

'I think I might get him this.' Robbo and Specky had wandered into a bookstore, and Robbo was holding up a book about footy legend Tony Lockett.

'Is this gift for you or for your dad?' asked Specky, smirking.

'For Dad, what d'ya reckon?' said Robbo.

'Do you think Lockett's a legend because of his dad? I bet *his* father loved footy.'

Robbo looked confused. He wasn't sure what Specky was getting at. 'Yeah, um, sure,' he replied.

Specky watched his friend walk over to the counter to purchase the book. For a moment, he wished *he* was the one buying a gift like that for his father. It would be really cool to flip through the pages of a footy book with Dad, he thought. That would never happen though.

Specky and Robbo made their way back to Robbo's house. Once there, they grabbed Robbo's Sherrin and headed out onto the quiet tree lined street for a friendly kick-to-kick.

'So, did you find any other pictures?' asked Robbo.

He booted the ball to Specky, who marked it on his chest.

'No, just the one.'

Specky kicked the footy back. Robbo fumbled, letting the ball drop to the road.

'Car!' yelled Specky.

Both he and Robbo strolled over to the footpath, to let the vehicle pass.

'Let me have a look again,' shouted Robbo.

'What?' asked Specky.

'Let me look at the picture again.'

Specky made his way over to Robbo and handed him the photograph.

Robbo squinted his eyes so he could thoroughly examine the photo.

'What? What are you trying to look for?' asked Specky, looking over Robbo's shoulder.

'Was this picture taken at your house?'

'No, it looks like someone else's, we don't have yellow walls,' said Specky. 'Why?'

'Did you notice that in the background there's a photograph hanging on the wall? It looks like a portrait of a couple or something, but it's too small to see it clearly. I bet whoever is in that picture is probably the owner of the house, *and* the person who took this photo.'

Specky screwed up his face at Robbo. 'When did you become Sherlock Holmes?'

'Look, I'm just trying to help. If you don't ...'

'No, no, I do!' said Specky. 'It's just too bad we can't see the background more clearly.'

'Maybe we can,' said Robbo. 'Follow me.'

Specky followed Robbo back into his house, and they made their way into Robbo's father's study.

'Give me your photo,' said Robbo. 'I'm going to scan it, then put it on the computer screen.'

Specky watched as Robbo swiftly operated his father's super-advanced computer equipment. Robbo's dad was a graphic designer, so he always had the latest stuff.

'There you go.' mumbled Robbo. Robbo had successfully managed to transfer the baby image of Specky onto the computer screen. 'Now all we have to do is enlarge the background section.' With a few clicks of the mouse, Robbo blew up the image.

'Oh man, I thought it would work. Sorry, Speck.'

Unfortunately, when the image was enlarged, it was very blurry. Specky could make out the shape of a man and woman's head but couldn't exactly see their faces.

'That's all right, thanks for trying,' said Specky, somewhat disappointed.

'Why don't you ask your dad about the picture?'

'Yeah, I s'pose I should. I hope it doesn't freak him out like it did Mum.'

'Well, if it does, then you know for sure they're hiding something from you. Maybe they really love footy and they just don't want to admit it,' said Robbo.

'Yeah right!' scoffed Specky. 'In my dreams! Nah, it's something else ... but what?'

For the rest of the afternoon, Specky and Robbo listened to the AFL games on the radio. In particular they liked listening to Rex Hunt. They loved the way he would make any game sound so exciting! Occasionally they paused to play some computer games, but Specky couldn't concentrate — his thoughts kept turning back to the photograph.

Eventually, Specky left Robbo's house and headed home. When he walked through the front door, he was surprised to see his father and mother seated together on the couch. It looked as if they had been waiting for him.

'How are you, son?' asked Specky's father nervously.

'I'm fine,' answered Specky, in a confused tone. There was an awkward pause between Specky and his parents. The way they stared at one another without saying a single word was very strange. Specky could tell that his parents had been discussing something quite serious before he walked in. And by the looks on their faces, it was obvious that the discussion was about him.

'Well, if that's all, I've got things to do,' Specky said as he quickly thumped up the stairs to the study, where he hopped in front of the computer and logged on.

Specky chewed at his fingernails as he waited for the phone line to connect.

That was really weird, thought Specky. He was totally baffled by his parents' odd behaviour.

Specky clicked his way into a football chat room, and a message appeared on the screen. It was from CHRISkicks.

CHRISkicks: Hey!

FOOTYHEAD: Hey!

CHRISkicks: The Blues won! Did all your teams win?

FOOTYHEAD: Um ... I think so.

CHRISkicks: What did you do this afternoon?

Specky decided to tell his online friend everything about the photograph, how his family were a non-football family, and how he missed kicking a goal that day. He practically told this complete stranger his entire life story.

CHRISkicks: Wow! That's some story.

FOOTYHEAD: Yeah, well, sorry I bored you.

CHRISkicks: No, you didn't. Weird, about that photo. Hey, did you ever wonder if you were adopted?

CHRISkicks: Hello?

CHRISkicks: Are you there?

CHRISkicks: HELLO???

Specky froze. Being adopted hadn't even crossed his mind until that very moment. He gasped and whispered to himself, 'That's it. Maybe I'm adopted?'

6

QUESTION TIME

Specky abruptly ended his conversation with CHRISkicks and shut down the computer. The thought of being adopted wasn't to be taken lightly. Specky wasn't sure how he would feel if it turned out to be true.

He went into his bedroom and nervously kicked his soft toy football around, bouncing it off the walls.

Specky started to wonder who his real parents were if he was adopted. And why did they get rid of him? It would explain a lot of things, though, like why he was so good at footy and his dad wasn't.

Specky suddenly had another thought. He took out the photograph from his pocket and stared at it again.

He decided that his *real* dad must have taken the picture and that *he* was the one who wrote on the back of it. Maybe he barracked for Geelong, which would mean that he loves footy, too. And maybe he was a champion player himself, and that was where Specky got his talent from.

Specky grinned to himself as he fantasised about the endless possibilities of having a dad who loved footy. Then he snapped out of it and his smile vanished.

This is crazy, he thought. He couldn't be adopted. He loved his mum and dad. They were his *real* parents.

Specky shoved the photograph into his sock drawer, determined to forget the whole thing, believing he was just being foolish to even consider such a thought. But that was easier said than done. For the next week, Specky went about his usual everyday business. He attended school, did his homework, watched his favourite TV shows, went to football training, and hung out with Robbo and Danny. But as hard as he tried, he couldn't keep his mind off the photograph and the idea that he could be adopted.

'Hey, Alice, can I ask you something?' Specky said as he entered his sister's room.

'What? Can't you see I'm on the phone!' she snapped. Alice was always on the phone. She lived on it. 'Hang on, my little brother is annoying me again,' she said to the person on the other end, then pressed the phone up against her chest. 'What? What do you wanna ask me? This better not be another lousy footy question.'

Specky cleared his throat. He was going to ask his sister straight out about the possibility of being adopted. If anyone knew anything to do with family matters, she did. Alice knew everything about everyone, he thought.

'Um, well, it's about ...'

'What? Hurry up! I haven't got all day. What's your question?'

Specky felt pressured by his sister and decided to change his question at the last second.

'Um, can you remember when I was born and when Mum brought me back from the hospital?' he asked.

Alice let out a huge annoyed huff. 'You've got to be kidding! I was only two years old when you were born. Honestly, how should I know? You were always there following me, getting in the way — like now! So if you have

44

no more questions, get lost! I'm only talking to the *hottest* guy in school.'

Specky left Alice's room and pondered his sister's answer.

'Well, maybe I'm not adopted. And if I was, then she definitely doesn't know a thing about it,' he concluded.

7

SENSATIONAL SPECKY!

Saturday morning arrived and Specky was scoffing down his breakfast. He was rushing to get ready for another footy game with his school team.

'Slow down or you'll choke!' said Specky's dad, who was reading the morning papers, which he had spread out across the table.

'So Dad, you think you might see me play today, catch the last quarter maybe?' said Specky hopefully, as he gulped down the last spoonful of his cereal.

'Sorry?' Specky's dad looked at him blankly.

It was obvious that his father had forgotten that today was the day that Coach Pappas was going to hold a mid-season barbecue after the game, in honour of the team's parents. Specky had told his dad a few weeks back about the event.

'Oh yes, yes, I remember. What time is that again? Yes, I'll try to be there for the barbecue but I can't be sure if I'll make it to see you actually play. And we won't be able to stay long at the barbecue either. You know this is a big day for me. I've got the launch of the Vladimir Belsky exhibition later this afternoon.'

Specky gave his father a questioning look as if to say, Vladimir who?

'You know, Vladimir Belsky the world-famous Russian sculptor. It's taken me years to get him and his work down here to Australia. There's going to be press, photographers — everyone. Which reminds me, take some good clothes with you to change into after the game. I'll pick you up and then we'll head straight to the gallery. Your mother and sister will meet us there. This is going to be a great day for all of us.'

Yeah, it would be an even better day if you came to see me play, thought Specky. He forced himself to smile back at his father, deeply hoping that, Russian sculptor or not, this wish would come true.

When Specky got to the school oval he was greeted by his team-mates and Coach Pappas.

'Alright, boys, warm-up time. I don't want any of you doing yourself an injury 'cause you haven't loosened up properly.'

Specky and his team-mates did their usual interval sprints and stretching until they were ready for the game to begin.

Specky made his way to the goal square. He was chosen to play full-forward again, and was determined to make amends for last week's game.

'Okay, focus, no thinking of Dad, the photo, or anything other than the game,' Specky said to himself.

The other team made their way onto the oval. Specky's opponent marched his way over towards him. Specky went to shake his opponent's hand as he did at the beginning of every match, to wish the other team a good game.

But this particular full-back was having none of it. 'Yeah, whatever!' he sneered, ignoring Specky's sportsman like gesture.

'Great, another one,' Specky mumbled to himself.

Just then the umpire blew his whistle and held the ball aloft to signal the beginning of the game.

He bounced the ball hard against the centre of the turf and the game began. Robbo was the first to get his clenched fist to the ball. He punched it long and direct to one of Specky's team-mates. Coach Pappas and the parents, who were standing either side of the oval, cheered. It was a great start for Booyong High.

In less than a minute the ball had already made its way down to the forward-line. Specky tussled with the full-back as the ball was kicked in his direction. The full-back grabbed hold of Specky's jumper, deliberately not letting him break away. The umpire quickly spotted this unfair play and sharply blew on his whistle. He awarded Specky the free kick. Specky's opponent protested and swore at the umpire.

'Another outburst like that from you, and you'll be sent off the ground!' warned the umpire.

Specky knew how hard it was to umpire a game. He had volunteered to umpire an Under 8 Auskick game earlier in the year and couldn't believe how difficult it was to make split-second decisions. He made a promise to himself that he would never argue with the umpire and would always accept their

decision whether he thought it was right or wrong. Specky thought that some of the AFL players who argued with the umpire looked silly and childish, and he suspected that they only did this as a way of covering up their own mistakes.

Specky went back to take his free kick. He was positioned in the same place as he had been the week before, when he had missed his chance of getting the winning six points. But this time there was no room for mistakes. Specky punted the ball directly through the middle of the big sticks.

For the rest of the first quarter and for the rest of the game, Specky's team trampled all over the opposition, Tremont High Tigers. Their ball handling and team skills were simply far superior.

As for Specky, he was on fire. He was playing the game of his life. He had already kicked an incredible twelve goals and there were still ten minutes remaining in the last quarter. Tremont High did everything they could to stop him. They even resorted to playing dirty, keeping in line with their reputation. They tried to trip, punch and injure Specky in any way they could. But Specky was too nimble and agile for them all. He ducked, twisted and turned, avoiding all their dirty tactics. None of them could lay a hand on him.

It was times like this that he was thankful Coach Pappas had introduced skipping rope as part of their training. At first the boys complained that skipping was for sissies, but Specky soon realised that it really helped him with his fitness and kept him light on his feet during the game. He skipped for 10 minutes before and after training.

Specky glanced over towards the boundary line. He quickly looked for his dad — but there was no sign of him.

'Specky!' It was Danny signalling that the ball was on its way. He had just kicked it towards Specky. Once again, Specky made a remarkable dash for it. He then athletically leaped for the ball like some World Cup soccer goalie, grabbing it securely with the tips of his fingers then sliding across the damp grass on his stomach. Specky had successfully taken another mark.

He then got up, casually pulled up his socks, flipped the ball in his hands a couple of times then lined up his kick.

Chris Grant, the Western Bulldogs Captain, had once come to Specky's school and conducted a football clinic, and had spoken about the importance of having a set routine when kicking for goal. You need to know exactly where the man on the mark will stand and how many paces you will take before you kick; the importance of keeping the ball still in your hands and over your kicking leg leading up to the kick; and the need to drop the ball straight onto your boot and finish with a strong follow-through. Specky also liked to pick out a target directly behind the goals, like a tree or a lamppost, to aim at. It sounded like a lot to remember at the time, but Specky had practised for hours each night, and now he was able to go through his routine without even thinking about it.

Before making contact with the ball, Specky took one last look over towards the boundary line. He wished his dad were there to see this at least.

But he wasn't. Specky took his kick, and booted his thirteenth goal for the game — a personal record. The umpire blew his whistle and the game was over. Specky's team-mates rushed to his side to congratulate him on his sensational performance, and to celebrate their convincing win.

8

MORE IMPORTANT?

Specky and his team-mates headed towards the parents and Coach Pappas. The portable barbecues were already set up, and Robbo's and Danny's fathers were turning the sizzling sausages and hamburgers. Specky scanned the crowd, hoping to see his father, but unfortunately he still hadn't arrived.

Once everyone had eaten, Coach Pappas got up to make an announcement.

'Welcome, everyone!' he began. 'It's great to see such a huge turnout. The boys should be happy that they have you supporting them. As you saw today, we have a great team this year, and I think we can go all the way.'

There was spontaneous applause and a cheer from everybody. Coach Pappas continued.

54

'Every year I have a tradition where I get each boy and one of his parents to participate in the annual mid-season barbie Longest Kick Competition. Every team member gets the chance to kick the ball as far as he can. Then we get one of his family members to also have a kick. And mums, it doesn't always have to be the dads who do the kicking. After everyone has had his or her kick, we tally up the measurement of both kicks. The family with the longest distance will win a great hamper full of gourmet goodies ...'

Everyone cheered again. Specky frantically looked back over his shoulder.

'Come on, where are you, Dad?' he said under his breath, not wanting to be left out.

Danny and his dad started off the competition, followed by Robbo and his father, then the rest of the team. There were some lousy, wobbly kicks and equally some terrific ones — but no matter how far the ball was booted, everyone was having fun.

Everyone but Specky. Specky was the only one in the team who didn't have a family member representing him. Coach Pappas and Robbo's dad offered to be his partner, but Specky politely declined. This scene was all too familiar for him. Specky couldn't help but be reminded of another time when he was so embarrassed. It was when he was eight. The Auskick team he was a part of organised a dads versus sons game. Each boy was to play directly against his own father. Unfortunately, Specky's dad was nowhere to be seen. So he was forced to play opposite Mrs Kavensky, the sausage sizzle lady and a former Olympian shot-putter who weighed over 100 kg. Specky was slaughtered by her, especially when she executed a 'hip and shoulder'! He felt so humiliated and now he found himself again not wanting his friends and coach feeling sorry for him.

Finally, everyone had had a kick and the friendly barbecue competition was over. Danny and his father had won. Specky congratulated his friend.

'Thanks. I'm sorry *your* dad wasn't here,' said Danny.

'That's okay. He doesn't know how to kick a football anyway,' Specky said with a brave smile.

Eventually Specky's team-mates, their parents and Coach Pappas headed home. Once again, Specky was left alone waiting for his dad to pick him up.

One hour later he finally arrived. Specky hopped into the passenger seat of the car, and slammed the door behind him.

'I'm so sorry, Simon. I just couldn't get away. I wanted to make sure Vladimir was comfortable, and the caterers needed direction. Anyway, the launch is all set to go and I got word today that the Premier of Victoria will be making an appearance. Isn't that exciting! Why aren't you out of your footy gear? You'll have to get changed on the way.'

Specky was fuming with anger, but he stopped himself from saying anything. He felt as if he was going to explode, especially since his father continued to ramble on about himself and the exhibition all the way to the gallery, without even noticing that Specky was upset.

An elderly lady with a big blonde hairdo shaped like a motorbike helmet, and who smelled of way too much perfume, rushed over to greet Specky's dad as they hopped out of the car and made their way into the gallery.

'Dar-ling! There you are! Where have you been? Who would've thought that they'd all come on time. The gallery is already full! Lady Jane, the Farrahs and Dame Stanistreet have all asked about you. And Vladimir is getting terribly anxious,' she said.

Specky's father hurriedly introduced her to him as the gallery's publicist, but the woman was far too caught up in herself and the event to acknowledge Specky. But he didn't care. As he mingled his way through the champagne-sipping crowd just behind his father, Specky heard a familiar voice.

'Hey, squirt!'

Specky turned to see it was Alice tapping him on the shoulder.

'You should let Dad go and do his schmoozing with everyone. Mum's over there keeping the Russian sculptor's wife company. She can't speak a word of English!'

Alice rolled her eyes then crossed her arms. She was totally unimpressed and bored by the whole event. Then she wandered off through the vast, white-walled gallery to get herself an orange juice from a nearby waiter, while Specky forced himself to check out the exhibition.

There were ten sculptures on display, each representing a part of the human body. They were all about a metre in height, and sat carefully on individual white podiums. What made the sculptures supposedly 'unique' was that they

were crafted entirely out of broken eggshells —
painstakingly glued together piece by piece.
Specky pushed his way to the front of the crowd
of art lovers to take a closer look. He stood
directly in front of a large eggshell nose. Specky
had to stop himself from laughing, especially
since everyone around him was so serious about
it. He couldn't help overhearing the conversation
of two ladies standing right beside him.

'You know, it takes him an entire year to
complete just one sculpture,' said one. 'This
piece alone is made of a thousand eggshells.
Now that's dedication.'

'And look at the realism of it all. The inner
strength it depicts, while at the same time
conveying a sense of vulnerability. That truly
speaks to me, Shantelle.'

'I know what you mean, Gloria. I also heard
that every egg was eaten by the sculptor
himself. But he's recently stopped doing that,
as he then began to suffer from major
constipation.'

Specky let out an uncontrollable 'huh!' and
giggled to himself some more.

The two ladies glared at Specky, unimpressed,
then turned and disappeared back into the
crowd.

'I did one just like that in my art class last term — I should've brought it along,' said an unfamiliar voice.

Specky turned to see who was talking to him. It was a boy about his age.

'Kind of dumb, isn't it?' the boy said, staring at the eggshell nose.

Specky nodded. 'Yeah, that's for sure. But I'd better not tell my dad what I think. He owns the place, that's my reason for being here. Why are you here?' Specky asked.

The boy who introduced himself simply as Greg, told Specky that he was with his father, who was an art collector. They were visiting from South Australia for the weekend.

'Hi, Greg. I'm Simon, but everyone calls me Specky. So do you barrack for the Crows or Port?' asked Specky, hoping that Greg knew his football.

'The Crows,' said Greg proudly. 'My dad and I are going to see them play tomorrow. I can't wait!'

'Your dad likes footy, then?'

'No, he hates it,' said Greg. 'But he'll go for me. Like I've come with him to this and I hate art. You like footy then?'

Specky nodded, not having really heard his

question. He was thinking how cool it was that this boy and his father supported each other in things that neither of them liked.

'Wanna have a kick now?' Greg asked Specky. 'I have a footy in our car outside.'

Specky didn't need to be persuaded — before he knew it he and Greg had left the boring exhibition launch and were having a kick-to-kick in the alleyway directly behind the gallery building.

After a few minutes of back and forth punting and marking, Greg said, 'How close do you think you can kick the ball to that open window up there?'

Specky grinned as he looked up at the window. It was about twenty-five metres from the ground. 'I bet I could get pretty close to it!' he said, ready for a little friendly competition.

Specky carefully aimed and booted the ball. The ball swished passed the window, and hit the wall about a metre above it.

'Too powerful! I have to pull back a bit! Here, you have a go,' said Specky, as the ball dropped back down to the ground.

Greg then took his turn but didn't get as close to the target as Specky's kick.

Both boys continued to take turns kicking the ball towards the open window, each time edging a little closer to it and declaring themselves the winner. Until Specky took his ninth try at it.

Thump! sounded the ball, as it left his foot and glided its way once again towards the target.

'Closer! Closer!' Specky said to himself in an effort to mentally push it along. 'This is going to be the closest. It looks as if it's going to get only centimetres away from it!' he grinned confidently.

Then, as if it had taken on a life of its own, and aided by an unexpected gust of wind, the ball floated through the open window and into the building.

The boys' jaws dropped.

'Oh no, it went in!' they shouted simultaneously. Specky and Greg continued to stare up at the window, nervously smiling, not sure what to do next. Moments later there came from inside a spine chilling *crash!* Then a number of screams, followed by complete silence and then ... '*S I M O N!!!*'

The boys suddenly turned to each other, the same horrified expression on both their faces.

'That was the window to the gallery!' they gasped.

9

THE TRUTH

Specky's first reaction was to run. If he could've left the country that very minute, he would have. But instead he decided to face the consequences. He and Greg reluctantly made their way back inside the building. As they entered the gallery, all heads turned directly to them. Specky caught sight of Alice and his mum first. Their faces were frozen in utter disbelief, like everyone else's. He looked towards the other end of the room to see that there, spread out on the floor, lay two very smashed sculptures, and in the middle of it all was the football he had accidentally just kicked through the open window. Thousands of tiny eggshell pieces were scattered all over the place.

Specky gulped as he then saw Vladimir Belsky sobbing on the floor while trying to pick up the remains of the sculpture called 'The Nose'.

'Come with me!' said Specky's father, grabbing him by the scruff of the neck and dragging him into his office.

'Dad, I didn't mean to . . .'

'Don't you dare say a single word,' hissed Specky's father through clenched teeth. He stormed off and slammed the office door shut behind him, leaving Specky to sit alone in the office for the rest of the launch.

By 7.00 p.m. the party was over — it really ended after the accident, as no one had been in the mood to celebrate since then.

Specky didn't move an inch or say a single word as he and his father drove home. He would've preferred to have got a lift back with his mum and Alice, but Specky's dad insisted that Specky go with him. Which only suggested to Specky that he was going to get an earbashing.

'That was supposed to be one of the biggest nights of my career and *you* ruined it! All I wanted was for my family to support me, to be there for me — even if it wasn't their thing . . .'

That's what I should be saying to you, thought Specky.

'. . . But no, my own son had to sabotage the whole event with his silly obsession with football.'

'It's not silly!' Specky answered back.

'Yes it is. I should ground you from playing footy for the rest of the year!'

'You can't do that! That's not fair! I didn't mean to break those sculptures . . .' Specky felt his entire face heat up and his eyes well with tears. 'Footy's my life, Dad, whether you like it or not. It's as important to me as art is to you. And you couldn't even make it to the barbecue today, at least I made an appearance at your stupid exhibition!'

'Don't you raise your voice at me, young man. Me not going to your football function is *not* the issue here!'

'Yes, it is! My *real* dad wouldn't have missed it!'

Specky's father suddenly slammed on the brakes, and the car screeched to a halt on the side of the road. Then he slowly turned to face Specky. 'What did you say?' he said firmly.

Specky gulped and quietly repeated himself, briefly regretting what he had just said. 'I said, my real dad wouldn't have missed the barbecue today.'

Specky's dad continued to stare at him in shock. After what seemed like a lifetime, he coldly turned back to the steering wheel and started the car.

Specky's heart was beating so fast, he felt as if he'd just sprinted the entire length of a football oval. Why wasn't his father saying anything? Part of Specky desperately wanted his father to say, 'Don't be silly, *I'm* your dad! What are you talking about?' — but he didn't.

For the remainder of the ride back home, the silence was deafening.

When Specky's dad pulled into their driveway, Specky quickly jumped out of the car, ran inside, and bolted up to his bedroom, slamming the door shut behind him. A minute later he could hear his father enter the house calling his wife's name. Specky lay quietly on his bed, trying to listen to his parents' conversation below. There was a lot of muffled mumbling coming from what sounded like the kitchen.

'Simon, come down here, please. Now! Your mother and I want to talk to you,' shouted Specky's dad.

Specky hesitantly made his way down the stairs, wishing he hadn't said what he did to his father.

'Sit down,' instructed his dad, who was sitting beside his mother in the lounge room.

Specky looked at his parents' faces — they seemed all squished with stress.

'Your mother and I weren't planning to tell you this until you were a little older. But in light of you finding the photo and what you just said to me in the car ...'

'Dad, I'm sorry about that, I ...' Specky wasn't quite sure if he was ready to hear what they were going to say.

'No, let me finish. We want you to know that we love you very much. You will always be our son, but we think you should know something. Something we never intended to keep from you.'

Specky's father looked back at his mother, then directly back at him. He took in a deep breath, and then spoke the words that Specky had suspected all along.

'You were adopted, son. You came into our lives soon after that photo you found was taken, and we are so blessed that you did. I am *still* your father and your mother is *still* your mother — we want you to understand that.

10

ADOPTED!

Specky couldn't help the sudden flood of tears that were streaming down his face. The realisation that he was adopted had hit him like a ton of bricks. His mother put her arm around him.

'If there's anything you want to know we'll tell you, okay? Please don't cry, Simon — you'll always be my boy!' She began to cry.

'But why didn't you tell me before this?' Specky asked, trying to hold back his tears.

'This isn't easy for us, Simon. I suppose we wanted to avoid it for as long as we could. Not to hurt you but to protect you. Your happiness is what's important to us.'

'Protect me from what? What do you mean? I can't believe this. How? Why?'

'Look ...' Specky's father stepped in. 'This is probably not the time to go into great details. It's been an emotional night for all of us.'

'Your father's right. Why don't you go and wash up and I'll get dinner ready, okay?'

Specky reluctantly agreed with his parents. It was all too much to take in right now. He wandered back up to his bedroom in a daze, and threw himself onto his bed, unaware that his beloved black cocker spaniel, Sammy, had followed him. Sammy jumped onto the bed and nestled in beside him.

'I knew, I knew it!' Specky sighed to himself.

'Can I come in?'

It was Alice tapping at Specky's bedroom door. Specky muttered 'no', but Alice entered anyway.

'I overheard it all, and I can't believe it either. Look, you're still my little brother and I'm still your sister, okay?'

Specky flopped his arm across his face. He didn't want Alice to see him tearing up again. Alice felt a little awkward. She wasn't sure what to say next.

'Um, the computer's free if you want it. I'll leave you to it then,' she said on her way out.

Specky decided to stay in his room until dinner was ready. An hour later, he made his way downstairs to find that the rest of the family had started eating without him.

'There you are! We thought you'd dozed off so we didn't want to disturb you. I kept your plate warm, sweetie,' said Specky's mum, acting all breezy, as if nothing major had happened.

Specky pulled up a chair and sat at the table, while his mum placed his dinner in front of him.

'There you go. Quick and simple but I know spaghetti and meatballs is one of your favourites.'

Specky couldn't help but suddenly feel like a stranger in his own home.

'So, Alice, how's that Geography homework of yours going?' asked Specky's father.

Alice screwed up her face — she hardly ever spoke about school to her parents. Specky could tell that his father was just trying to make conversation. Like his mother, he too was pretending that everything was fine. Specky couldn't take it anymore.

'So ...' he interrupted his father, 'who are my *real* parents then?'

Specky's mother fumbled with her knife and

fork, dropping them onto her plate. Alice nervously took a large gulp from her glass of water.

'*We're* your real parents, Simon,' answered Specky's dad firmly. 'We have been and always will be your parents. Today's news shouldn't change a thing.'

'Your father's right. Life should continue as it is,' added Specky's mother.

Specky wasn't satisfied with his parents' response. 'Do you know who they are? Where did you get me from?'

'If you mean your biological parents, no, we don't know who they are.' Specky's father shot a guilty look towards his mother. 'We got you through an adoption agency,' continued Specky's dad.

'Then who took the picture of me dressed up in footy gear?' asked Specky.

Again, Specky's father gave his mother a worried look.

'The agency gave it to us,' explained Specky's mother. Tiny beads of perspiration on her forehead and neck glistened in the light.

'Then why did you want to adopt me? Couldn't you have another one of your own, like Alice? Or is Alice adopted too?'

Alice almost choked on her food. 'Am I?' she squealed.

'No, you're not. The truth is ...' Specky's dad once again glanced back at Specky's mum. Her eyes were wide open, as if she was unsure exactly what Specky's father was about to say. 'The truth is that it just happened to be the right time for you to come into our lives. All we know is that your biological mother is dead — unfortunately, she was killed in a car accident. And we have no idea who your biological father is.'

Specky looked at his mum. She dropped her head so that Specky couldn't look her directly in the eye.

'You still haven't answered my question. Why did you want to adopt in the first place? And how do you know all this? You just said you didn't know who my real parents were.' It was obvious to Specky that there was more to the story than his parents were willing to tell him. Just then, his father abruptly pushed his chair away from the table and stood up.

'Look, Simon, I'm sorry you had to find out like this, but that's all we know. Enough questions. *We're* your parents and that's that! And after your performance at the gallery this afternoon, I wouldn't push it!' Specky's dad stormed out of the room, leaving Specky even more confused and upset.

'Your father didn't mean to shout, love. We just want you to know that we're here for you,' Specky's mother said softly. As she began clearing the table, Specky could see she was trying to hold back from crying again.

'Mum, can't you tell me more?'

Specky's mum firmly slammed down the plates on the table and this time stared directly into Specky's eyes. 'Simon, your father and I love you very much, that's all you need to know.' Specky's mum then turned and walked out of the room.

'Whoah, what a day this has been. Like something out of the twilight zone!' remarked Alice. 'I hate to say this, but they're right, you know. They're your — our — parents, Si. They're the ones who raised us and that's the only thing that should matter. I know you must be freaked out at the moment, but you really should just try to forget about it.'

Alice got out of her seat and left Specky to finish his dinner alone.

How can I just forget about it? he thought. I have another dad! Another dad, who obviously loves footy!

11

CHRISKICKS

On the following Monday morning at school, Specky still wasn't sure if he was going to share his news with his friends. It wasn't something he felt he wanted a lot of people to know.

'What's with you? You haven't said a word all morning. What's up?' asked Robbo during recess.

'Look, if I tell you, you have to keep it to yourself. Promise?' said Specky.

Robbo crossed his heart with his forefinger and gave an exaggerated nod.

'All right,' began Specky. 'Remember the photograph of me dressed up in all the Geelong gear? Well, I suspect my dad took it.'

'Your dad? But your dad isn't into footy and ...'

Specky took in a deep breath and stopped Robbo mid-sentence. 'No, not my dad that you know, my *biological* dad. I found out I'm ...' Specky took in another breath. It was still difficult to believe this was all happening. 'I'm adopted!'

Robbo paused for a few seconds before he fully understood what he had just heard. 'No way! You're *adopted*! What are you going to do? Are you going to look for them — your real parents, I mean?'

Specky shrugged his shoulders. He felt kind of relieved that he had told someone.

'Um, I don't know. I'm not sure if I want to. Where would I begin, anyway? My parents freaked out on me when I tried to find out more, so I know *they* won't help me. They told me my biological mother is dead, but my father is out there, somewhere.'

Robbo shook his head in disbelief, not really sure how to react. 'Man, you know what this means. Your dad, I mean, your biological dad, is probably into footy. That's why you were dressed in all that footy gear as a baby!'

'Oh derr, no kidding,' Specky replied sarcastically. 'I haven't stopped thinking about that since they told me.'

The bell sounded, and Specky and Robbo made their way back to class. By the end of the day it seemed that everyone in school knew about Specky's secret.

'I'm sorry, mate!' pleaded Robbo, running up to Specky near the front gates of the school.

'I thought I told you to keep it to yourself.'

'I did, but I thought it wouldn't hurt just to tell Danny, and then he thought he could tell ...'

'Look,' snapped Specky, 'it's okay. I don't care anymore. I just wish I had never found that stupid photo in the first place.'

Specky bolted away from Robbo, and ran nonstop all the way home. When he got there, his mother greeted him at the front door, offering home-made snacks — this was so out of the ordinary. Specky declined the food with a shake of the head and ran upstairs to log on to the computer. He didn't want to deal with anything or anyone. He wanted to totally forget about all this adoption stuff. Instead, all he wanted to do was get online and surf a few of his favourite footy sites. That'll provide the perfect distraction, he thought. After a few minutes online, Specky was messaged by CHRISkicks.

CHRISkicks: Hey! What happened to you the other day? You signed off in a rush.

FOOTYHEAD: Yeah, sorry about that. You were right.

CHRISkicks: Right? I was right about what?

FOOTYHEAD: About being adopted. My parents told me yesterday. It's true, I'm adopted.

CHRISkicks: Wow! How do you feel?

FOOTYHEAD: It's a weird feeling, hard to explain.

CHRISkicks: I know what you mean.

FOOTYHEAD: What do you mean you know? How could you possibly know how I feel?

CHRISkicks: 'Cause I'm adopted, too!

Specky wondered if this was a joke. Now he was more curious than ever to find out more about this 'CHRISkicks' kid. Up until now, he was happy just to talk footy with him. But that had changed — now they had something more in common than just Aussie Rules.

FOOTYHEAD: So how long have you known you were adopted?

CHRISkicks: I've known for a long time. Since I was able to talk. My parents are the coolest people around. I consider my adopted parents to be my real parents.

FOOTYHEAD: Do you ever wonder about your real parents though? Would you ever look for them?

CHRISkicks: Why? Do you want to search for your biological parents?

Specky took in another deep breath. He couldn't deny the fact that deep down, he had a burning desire to find out more about his *other* father. I wonder if he can kick booming torpedoes. I bet he can! he fantasised.

CHRISkicks: Hello? Are you still there?

FOOTYHEAD: Yeah, I'm here. Sorry.

CHRISkicks: Don't let this adoption thing freak you out too much. If you want to chat some more about it, I don't mind.

FOOTYHEAD: Thanks.

CHRISkicks: That's okay. So how are all your AFL
    teams going?

FOOTYHEAD: I'm not sure. I haven't paid much
    attention lately.

CHRISkicks: Well, I'm going to the G this weekend
    to see the Geelong vs Collingwood match!

FOOTYHEAD: Really? I'm going to be there this
    weekend too!

Specky and Robbo had been invited to the
match a few weeks ago by Danny and his family.
Danny had been talking about it all week.

FOOTYHEAD: But why are you going to see that
    game? I thought you barracked for the Blues?

CHRISkicks: I do, but my dad will be working there
    this weekend, so I'm tagging along.

FOOTYHEAD: Working at the footy? Doing what?

FOOTYHEAD: Hello? You there?

CHRISkicks: Sorry, Mum distracted me. She's telling me to log off. She wants to use the phone line. Hey, do you want to meet up?

FOOTYHEAD: Um, well, I'm not sure.

CHRISkicks: That's cool, it's up to you. Only if you want.

Specky paused for a second before typing an answer. He knew it was definitely a dumb thing to arrange to meet a total stranger from an online chat room. There was no way he would ever do that. But he thought it would be safe because he was going to be with friends, and in a public place.

FOOTYHEAD: Okay, I'll be in the Members Stand. Can you meet me there?

CHRISkicks: Yeah, I can do that. Where exactly?

FOOTYHEAD: I'll meet you directly in front of the Barassi Bar at half-time. I think it's between entrance 23 and 24, but I'm not 100 per cent sure. I'll be wearing a baseball cap. It's navy

blue, like the one Tiger Woods wears. My mates
Robbo and Danny will probably be with me.

CHRISkicks: Cool, I'll see you then. See ya!

FOOTYHEAD: Wait! How will I recognise you? And
you forgot to tell me what sort of work your
dad will be doing at the game?

FOOTYHEAD: Hello?

CHRISkicks had already logged off. Specky
was left to think about what he had just
committed to.

For the rest of the week, he went about his
life as normally as possible. He hadn't told
anyone, not even Robbo or Danny, about his
planned meeting with CHRISkicks. He felt it
best not to say a word, not until they were at
the game. He didn't want it to somehow get
back to his parents that he was going to meet a
kid who could possibly help him search for his
other father — his 'footy father'.

12

SIMMO

Finally Saturday arrived, and Specky was once again playing football for his school, this time against a team called Redleaf College Rovers. It was half-time and Booyong High were gathered around Coach Pappas.

'Okay, boys, great first half. But just because we're four goals in front doesn't mean we can slacken off now. Speck, I reckon I'll put you on the wing for the second half. Swap with Simmo.'

Everyone's jaws dropped in unison. They were gobsmacked — some of them almost choked on their quartered oranges and bottled water. What did the coach think he was doing? Their number one goal scorer on the wing? And Michael 'Simmo' Simpson at full-forward? It was pure craziness. For starters, the whole team, including Simmo, knew he wasn't exactly a strong marking type. In fact, he wasn't much of a kick, either. But that's not to say he wasn't liked by his fellow players — he was. He was a respected team player, and was passionate about his footy, but Coach Pappas's decision to position him in the goal square in place of Specky was a strange one indeed.

Specky, Robbo and Danny couldn't help but notice that there was one person who was extremely happy with the switch — Simmo's dad. He smiled proudly and gave the Coach a big wink of approval.

'Did you see that?' whispered Danny to Specky. 'That stinks! My dad would never tell the Coach where to play me!'

Specky had to agree with Danny. It looked as if the Coach's decision had been influenced by Simmo's dad. And if that was the case, then it was totally out of character for the Coach.

Coach Pappas hadn't been persuaded by bossy parents in the past, so why would he be now? But then Simmo's dad could hardly be considered a bossy parent — he was actually a very pleasant man and a loyal supporter of the team. This made the sudden switch all the more unusual.

As Specky wandered back out onto the oval towards the wing position, Simmo ran up alongside him.

'Specky. I hope y-y-y-you d-d-don't mind.' Simmo had a stutter, and it seemed to get a little worse when he was nervous. 'I-I-I didn't mean to t-t-take your p-p-p-position. It's just that m-m-my d-d-dad is . . .'

'Simmo, it's cool. Relax. I don't care, really.' But Specky did care. He couldn't help thinking that if his biological 'footy dad' were there, he would've protested against Coach Pappas's decision.

Simmo wanted to fully explain why his father did what he did, but once again Specky cut him off.

'Look, Simmo, forget it. You'd better get to your *new* position, the quarter is about to start,' he said.

Simmo ran off to take up his place at full-forward. 'S-s-s-sorry!' he shouted back over his shoulder to Specky.

But Specky wasn't having any of it. Even though it wasn't in his nature to be resentful, he still couldn't help feeling slightly annoyed. He looked over towards Danny and Robbo and rolled his eyes.

The first ball of the third quarter was bounced, and immediately Specky's team-mates had control of the ball, and moved it down into their forward-line. The forward pocket player for Specky's team, Sanjay 'The Bombay Bullet' Sharma (nicknamed this by his mates because he had recently migrated from India and was a super-fast sprinter) took a safe mark and then beautifully kicked the ball towards Simmo. Unfortunately, Simmo fumbled and dropped the ball, missing the easiest of chest-marks. The full-back for Redleaf College swooped in and capitalised on Simmo's blunder, darting off with the ball. He had a large opening ahead of him and decided to make a heroic dash. Specky's team was caught off guard by the surprise break away.

You need to have confidence to run and carry the football. Bouncing the ball at top speed can be difficult, and should be practised under pressure at training. Wherever possible, Specky and his mates always had a football in their hands. They would have competitions with one another while they ran their warm-up laps at training. How many times could they bounce the ball as they ran half a lap, flat out? Could they bounce the ball, on the run, with their non-preferred hand? Could they bounce two balls at the same time, one with the right hand and one with the left hand? These drills were designed to improve their ball handling.

Specky made a rush towards him, as did Danny. The full-back player bounced the ball once, then again and again. His team-mates gallantly shepherded him, providing a clear passage. He covered an enormous amount of ground, even crossing the centre line. It was rare for a full-back player to achieve such a feat, and Specky and his team-mates struggled to get a firm grip on him.

The full-back eventually kicked the ball into the safe hands of his team's full-forward. Coach Pappas was screaming from the sideline, disgusted by his team's sudden lapse of concentration. Redleaf's full-forward carefully lined up his kick, tested the wind by throwing a handful of grass in the air, and shot for goal — it soared right through the middle.

As the ball was escorted by the boundary umpire back to the centre, Specky and his team-mates shook their heads in frustration.

Once again, the ball was bounced and Specky's team-mates, determined to make amends, quickly got it down to their forward-line. But what happened next was almost an identical repeat of the previous play. That is, Simmo again missed an easy mark, the full-back took advantage of his mistake, made a break away, ran for most of the entire ground, and kicked the ball to his full-forward, who scored another goal — all in the span of just a few minutes.

The Redleaf Rovers were on a roll, and continued to outplay Specky's team for the entire quarter. By the sound of the umpire's whistle, they had not only clawed their way back, but had taken the lead by one clear goal. Specky's team-mates were quick to blame Simmo for their dismal quarter. Every goal the other team had kicked was indirectly a result of Simmo's bad play.

'So, are you going to switch Specky back to full-forward?' chorused some of the boys to Coach Pappas as they gathered round for the third-quarter address.

Specky glanced over at Simmo, who dropped his head in embarrassment. Simmo couldn't face anyone. He was very upset — he knew he was letting down the entire team. Specky suddenly felt kind of sorry for him. And he also felt slightly guilty that he and the rest of the team were being a little hard on him.

Coach Pappas wasn't impressed, to say the least.

13

HIS DREAM . . .

'How dare you all assume that the reason you're losing is solely because of one player! This isn't the team I know. Now stop being so petty — all of you! Great footy players are versatile. They can play in all positions if needed, and it's a team that wins the game, not just one player. Now get out there and show me teamwork, instead of being such a bunch of whingeing babies pointing the finger at one another!' Coach Pappas stormed back to the boundary line and joined the parents and other supporters.

'Come on, everyone, he's right! We can win this!' shouted Robbo, who was doing his best to encourage and motivate everyone.

Some players, when things are going against them or their team, retreat into their shells and go all quiet. Real leaders stand out when things aren't going well. They handle pressure better and look upon the situation as a challenge. Not everyone is comfortable being a leader, using their voice to motivate those around them. Some people prefer to let their actions do the talking for them. But leadership is invaluable, and Robbo was a natural whom the whole team looked up to.

The team eagerly jogged back to their positions, ready to begin the final quarter. Specky took up his position on the wing, right next to where the coach and parents were standing. He glanced over to see Coach Pappas patting Simmo's dad on the back. From a distance, Simmo's father appeared very appreciative that the coach had continued to leave his son in the full-forward position. Specky was still baffled by their alliance, but somehow sensed that there must be more to this than plain favouritism.

Whatever the real reason, Specky didn't have time to think about it — the quarter had started. And what a quarter it turned out to be. It was a hard slog for both teams. Booyong High had regained the excellent skills they had shown in the first half of the game, while Redleaf College were still on the same lucky roll they displayed in the previous quarter. It was goal for goal all the way. Robbo, Danny and Specky all kicked one each, while 'The Bombay Bullet' evened the scores with superb back-to-back snaps from both pockets.

It was no surprise to anyone that 'The Bombay Bullet's' two favourite AFL players were Geelong's Ronnie Burns and the former Melbourne 'Wizard', Jeff Farmer, now with the Fremantle Dockers. Like these two stars, the 'Bullet' had exceptional goal sense, and was always able to find the 'big sticks', regardless of how much pressure he was under. He could kick superb 'bananas' from the boundary or dribble them through along the ground with the ball turning like a Shane Warne leg spinner. Like his two heroes, 'The Bombay Bullet' loved to kick goals — running cartwheels and several back flips were his preferred methods of celebration.

There was only a minute or so of the game left to go, and scores were still level.

'I'm free!' yelled Specky, rushing towards an open space right by the edge of the centre square.

Paul Solomon, known to the rest of Specky's team as 'Smashing Sols' for his hard-hitting tackles, had possession of the ball. He drop-kicked it directly into Specky's chest. Specky knew he didn't have the time to pull up his socks and execute a controlled kick. Instead, he played on, twisting and baulking his way towards the forward-line.

 We all know that footy is a physical game, and 'Smashing Sols' loved nothing more than laying a big tackle or delivering a tough, fair bump. His dad, a former legend of the local Eastern Suburbs League who was renowned as one of the toughest players ever to pull on a footy boot, was always telling him that you only got hurt in football if you put in a half-hearted effort. 'Sols' never went at the ball half-heartedly, and he never got hurt.

Rushing over from the other team to knock Specky off his feet was a fierce-looking back-pocket opponent.

Fortunately, Specky caught a glimpse of him before there was any chance of the two of them colliding. He delicately hand-balled over his opponent's head into the hands of Danny, who was running all over the ground, as a good rover should. Specky gracefully side-stepped the back-pocket player and continued to run forward. Danny then hand-balled the ball back to Specky. It was a brilliant fast-action one-two manoeuvre by the two friends.

A lot of young players don't like to hand-ball, preferring to kick the ball at every opportunity. But used effectively , hand-balling it can create many goal opportunities. Danny and Specky had a great understanding on the field, and often found themselves hand-balling to each other. Each night, after training was finished, they would hand-ball the ball to each other 100 times, with both their left and right hands, before they went home. During the game they mainly used low, flat hand-balls that spun backwards through the air, like a drop punt — these were called 'rocket hand-balls'. They could also float hand-balls over their opponents' heads, and could even hand-ball along the

*ground to each other if they were caught in
the middle of a pack.*

Specky took a bounce, looked up, and saw
he was still too far out to kick a goal. The only
team-mate who was free and available for him
to boot the ball onto was Simmo. Specky had
no choice but to kick it to him. The ball drifted
high into the sky, directly above the clumsy
full-forward. Simmo's knees rattled with
nerves, while sweat trickled down the back of
his neck. The full-back for Redleaf, who'd left
Simmo in order to chase the ball, was now
charging back towards him. Specky and the rest
of his team anxiously looked on, hoping Simmo
wouldn't blow it again.

'Come on, Simmo, you can mark this one.
You can do it,' muttered Specky under his breath.

Just as the ball was in his reach, Simmo
closed his eyes, took a deep breath and hoped
for the best. Redleaf's full-back took a huge
leap and dived towards Simmo, grabbing him
around the neck. The ball slipped through
Simmo's fingers as he and the full-back went
crashing down to the ground. The umpire blew
his whistle, and awarded Simmo a free kick,
directly in front of goal.

Coach Pappas, the supporters and Specky's team all let out a huge sigh of relief. Specky sprinted over to Simmo to give him some words of encouragement before he took his kick.

'Don't be nervous, mate. Do it for your dad,' he whispered into his ear. Specky wasn't sure why he said what he had, but by the touched expression on Simmo's face, he knew he had somehow said the right thing.

Simmo lined up his kick, glanced over to his father (who gave him a proud nod), then aimed for the goal. The ball went right through the centre of the goal posts as the umpire blew his whistle to signal that the game was over. Specky's team had won another match, but only just.

Back in the changing rooms, Coach Pappas took Specky aside.

'I'm very proud of you today, Speck. I noticed you settled Simmo's nerves out there. It was very good of you, especially since I know you would've preferred it if I'd kept you at full-forward. There's a reason I switched you with Simmo today.'

The Coach looked around to see if anyone else was listening. Nobody was. Danny and Robbo were flicking towels at 'The Bombay

Bullet' and 'Smashing Sols', while Simmo was getting a huge hug from his dad. Coach Pappas continued.

'The reason is, Simmo's father recently found out he's got cancer, and Monday he begins chemotherapy. This will last for weeks, possibly months. Anyway, he won't be able to come out and see Simmo play footy again — not for a while, at least — so he asked if I could put him at full-forward. His dream was to see his boy kick a goal, and he got his wish, thanks to you. You helped make that happen.'

Specky now felt guiltier than ever for originally thinking that Simmo's dad and Coach Pappas were involved in some kind of match-fixing conspiracy. He was glad and relieved that things had turned out the way they had.

'So, are ya ready? Maggies, here we come!' shouted Danny.

He and Robbo had ended their towel fight and were now eagerly waiting for Specky to get changed.

'Hurry up, Speck. Dad's waiting for us in the car!'

In no time at all, Specky was ready and seated beside his friends in Danny's father's four-wheel drive. As he strapped his seat belt on, he noticed Simmo and his dad waving to him as they made their way across the parking lot. Simmo mouthed the words 'thank you'. Specky smiled and gave him a thumbs-up in return. Danny and Robbo hadn't noticed.

'Carn the Pies!' shouted Danny.

'Here we go, here we go, here we go!' chanted Robbo.

The two whooped and whistled. They were bursting with excitement, while Specky quietly continued to observe Simmo and his father from afar.

He imagined for a moment what they'd say to each other on the way home, and how Simmo's father would be so proud of him — proud of his son playing footy. Specky sighed as he watched them get into their car and drive off.

He turned his attention back to his friends. Now it was his turn to get excited — he was off to the MCG!

14

MAGNIFICENT MCG

It dawned on Specky that the last time he had visited the hallowed home of Aussie Rules — the Melbourne Cricket Ground — was at least a couple of years ago, and that time he had also been with Danny Castelino and his family.

'Okay, okay, settle down!' ordered Danny's father from behind the steering wheel.

Danny and Robbo were getting a little out of hand in the back seat, belting out the anthems of their footy teams at passing traffic. Danny's younger brother, Phillip, sat in the front passenger seat and was giggling at his brother's antics. Specky smiled. He loved hanging out with Danny and his big Italian family. They were all die-hard Collingwood supporters — actually, they were avid fans of most sports.

Specky remembered staying overnight at Danny's place one time and they hadn't gone to bed until five in the morning — Danny and his family were all up watching the World Cup Soccer, telecast live from overseas. He had so much fun watching Danny's dad, uncles and cousins jumping up and down around the lounge room every time Italy kicked a goal. It was certainly a different world from his family. This made him wonder about his biological dad again.

Dad and I would *never* stay up all night and watch a sporting event together, but I bet my other dad would, Specky mused.

Danny's father pulled into the parking lot of the MCG. They all hopped out and joined the flocks of fans who were spilling out from the Richmond train station across the road. Specky stared in awe at the giant stadium as he and his friends made their way towards the AFL members' entrance gates. Seeing this larger-than-life national landmark sent a tingle all the way down Specky's spine.

'One day I'll play here,' he promised himself, under his breath.

Danny's father generously paid for Robbo's and Specky's tickets, and they all excitedly clicked their way through the turnstiles. Once inside, Specky followed Robbo, Danny, and Danny's brother and father through the vast concrete hallway. There was an air of excitement brewing as fans decked out in their team's colours dodged and passed one another on the way to their seats. Specky could hear a distant roar from inside the ground — it was the crowd that arrived earlier in the day, cheering during the last few minutes of the reserves' match.

'There it is,' said Danny proudly, as he and the others stood at the top of the aisle facing the immaculate green turf before them.

Specky grinned. 'Wow! I forgot how big it was,' he gasped, as he and the others made their way down to the front-row seats, close to the boundary line.

It was a gloriously sunny day, with just a hint of a winter breeze sweeping over the city side of the stadium — perfect for footy.

'Hey, about time you made it. I couldn't hold these seats any longer.' It was Danny's Uncle Joe and other members of the Castelino family. Specky edged his way in behind his friends as he and Robbo were introduced to everyone.

'Boys, you remember everyone here, don't you?' said Danny's dad.

Specky and Robbo nodded.

There was Danny's Uncle Joe, his Uncle Santo, his younger cousins Stefan, Luisa, Jayden and family friends Ron and his son Adrian.

Specky waved a friendly hi to them all — he still couldn't get over how they *all* loved footy. He briefly fantasised about what it would be like if he, his parents and Alice were all there together.

'Hey, Speck. Snap out of it, man.' It was Danny nudging Specky to stop daydreaming. 'That official over there is trying to get your attention, Speck. He's pointing directly at you.'

Specky looked up to see that there was indeed an official-looking person standing on the boundary pointing at him. He waved Specky over to the fence.

'Hey, kid!' he said. 'Do you want to play Superbikes, the giant-screen computer game? I've already chosen a kid who supports Geelong. Are you a Collingwood supporter?'

Before Specky had a chance to explain to the man that he barracked for five teams, Danny quickly answered for him.

'Yes, he is. And he'll play the game.'

'Great!' said the official.

Specky wasn't sure if he wanted to play. He felt a little pressured.

'Come on, Speck, this is all part of the pre-game entertainment. They always pick kids out of the crowd. I've wanted to get picked for ages. Come on, you might win something really cool!' urged Danny.

'Yeah, and Superbikes is really easy. You've played it on my computer tons of times,' added Robbo.

Specky agreed and jumped over the fence to join the official and his competitor. They then made their way over to the other side of the ground, where a portable PlayStation was set up. The official grabbed a microphone and spoke to the crowd.

'Okay, ladies and gentlemen, we're ready for another game of Superbikes!' His voice echoed throughout the entire stadium.

Specky looked up to see that his face and the computer game's graphics were up on the giant

TV screen for everyone to see. He and the other boy were each handed a joystick.

'All right,' continued the official. 'We have Luke representing Geelong ...'

There was an instant roar from all the Geelong supporters.

'And we have ...' The official leaned away from the microphone and asked for Specky's name. Specky almost said Simon, but then decided to say Specky.

'And we have Specky — yes, you've heard right, ladies and gentlemen — Specky, who'll be hoping to take a specky for Collingwood.'

Then there was an equally large cheer from all the Collingwood supporters.

'Yeah, Speck! Go the Pies!' shouted Danny and his family.

'Okay Specky, you're player one, and Luke, you're player two. Take your marks ... GO!'

Specky pushed his joystick forward and fumbled slightly with the other controls as he stared intensely at the small monitor in front of him. He concentrated on the tiny bike graphics as they twisted and turned around an animated racing track. He could tell from the frantic commentary given by the official that it was a close competition.

'It's neck and neck. Luke is slightly in front for Geelong. Look out for that wall, Specky! Whoa, that was close ...'

'Go, Specky, go!' cheered Robbo and Danny.

The official was becoming more and more excited as the two boys approached the end of the game.

'Specky's hit the lead! No, it's Luke! It's going to be hard to separate this one. And here comes the finishing line, and the winner is ...'

15

FAMILY, FRIENDS AND FANTASY

'And the winner is Luke, for Geelong! Congratulations, Luke. You and your dad will be off on a father-and-son footy camp, which will be hosted by some of your favourite AFL champs and Auskick. Specky, bad luck, mate. Hopefully Collingwood will play better today than you did — only joking!'

There was a loud groan of disapproval from the Collingwood cheer squad at the official's poor joke.

Specky was then escorted back to his seat.

'Don't worry, Speck. You did a great job,' said Danny's father.

'You were robbed, man!' added Danny and Robbo, patting Specky on the back as he sat down beside them.

Specky didn't mind losing one bit, once he heard what the prize was. He was sort of glad and relieved in a way. The thought of trying to convince his dad to join him at a footy camp was farcical, and it made him think once again of his biological father. I bet *he* would have been happy to go with me, thought Specky.

'Here they come! Wahooo!' Danny pointed to the Collingwood players, who had just started jogging out onto the field. The Magpie theme song was blasting loudly through the speakers across the ground, while fans cheered and applauded their entrance. The Geelong supporters couldn't help but boo and hiss at them.

The Collingwood cheer squad raised their giant banner, and struggled to hold it up in place. It read, 'Maggies: Ready to Swoop all over Kitty Cats!' There was another roar from the black-and-white barrackers as their beloved team charged the wall of paper and burst through it.

Specky looked up into the stands. He guessed the ground attendance had to be close to 80,000 people. It was like a finals game.

The Geelong team was next, bursting through their banner. It read, 'Minced Pies for Everyone!'

'Boooo! *You're* the ones that are mincemeat, Geelong!' hissed Danny's Uncle Joe.

Specky smiled to himself. He had forgotten how footy spectators could get so vocal at a live match — especially Danny's Uncle Joe.

'Come on! Get on with it. Let's crush this team!' he shouted, sipping from his can of cola.

Finally, the siren to signal the beginning of the game was sounded. There was a raucous roar from every single person in the stadium — the atmosphere was electric. Specky screamed out alongside his friends. He had goosebumps running up and down his arms. There was no other place in the world he would rather have been that afternoon.

The first quarter ended up a runaway success for Collingwood. They had kicked five goals two to Geelong's measly one goal one. Danny's family couldn't be more ecstatic. In the break they hurried to the toilets, stocked up on meat pies and drinks, and prepared themselves for the second quarter. It was during this period that Specky decided to tell Robbo and Danny about his planned meeting with CHRISkicks.

'Are you crazy?' asked Danny. 'It could be anyone, a real freak or something.'

'Yeah, I know, I know. That's why I'm telling you both. He's going to give me some information on adoption and stuff,' said Specky.

Specky's friends disapproved of his planned rendezvous with this so-called online friend, so they decided to tag along with him, just in case.

During the second quarter, Geelong made a minor comeback, bridging the score by only two goals the difference. Danny's family, as well as most of the Collingwood supporters, blamed it on the umpires.

'Get glasses, Ump!'

'No way, Ump! How much did they pay you!'

'You're blind, Ump!'

'How many freebies are ya gonna give 'em?'

By half-time, there were only five points separating the two teams, and Specky, Danny and Robbo scampered off to meet the CHRISkicks kid.

'So where is he?' asked Robbo impatiently.

The three boys were all hanging out around the entrance of the Barassi Bar, as planned.

'Well, maybe he thought *I* was some cyber freak. I told him to look out for my blue cap,' answered Specky.

Suddenly, Specky got a tap on the shoulder.

He turned to see an Asian girl, about his age, smiling at him.

'Are you *Footyhead?* Or should I say Specky — you were the one playing Superbikes, weren't you?' she asked.

'Yes, I am. But who are you?' asked a confused Specky.

'I'm CHRISkicks!'

'*You're* CHRISkicks?' Specky was blown away. He never thought that his online footy friend could be a girl.

'Yes, I am. My name is Christina. Chris for short — CHRISkicks!'

Robbo and Danny sniggered at each other. They could tell that Specky was shocked.

'Oh, and these are my friends, Emily and Sophie.' Christina introduced Specky to her friends. 'They tagged along, just in case you ended up being someone creepy ...'

Robbo and Danny chuckled again. Specky then introduced them to Christina and her friends.

'Anyway, here's that stuff I promised,' said Christina, as she handed over some pamphlets to Specky. 'There's a number in there you can call if you ever decide to search for your biological parents.'

'Um, thanks, thanks a lot.' Specky was still surprised. He couldn't get over the fact that all this time he had been chatting to a girl. And not just any girl, but a girl who was just as passionate about footy as he was. Christina could see that Specky felt more awkward about the whole situation than she did, so she tried to make friendly conversation.

'So, are you guys enjoying the footy? You reckon Collingwood will win?'

'You bet!' quipped Danny. Robbo nudged Danny in the ribs. He knew that the question was directed to Specky.

'Y-y-y-yeah, I am,' stuttered Specky. 'So, where are you sitting?'

'I'm up in the corporate boxes,' replied Christina.

Specky glanced over to his friends. They raised their eyebrows at him — they were impressed.

Christina continued. 'Yeah, my dad's a TV director — he directs a lot of the televised matches.'

Specky couldn't contain himself. 'Wow, that's what you meant by him working here. That's so cool!'

No one was sure what to say next.

'Um, well, it was nice meeting you, Specky. I'll see you online sometime,' said Christina.

'Yeah, okay,' mumbled Specky.

Christina and her friends turned and headed back towards their seats.

'Oh, and thanks again for these!' yelled Specky, holding up the pamphlets.

Christina glanced back over her shoulder and waved. Specky watched her disappear into the crowd, feeling totally gobsmacked.

16

SPECKY'S SEARCH

Robbo and Danny couldn't help stirring Specky about his reaction to meeting Christina.

'A girl, huh! You should have seen your face, Specky,' teased Danny.

'Yeah, it was so red, just like it is now. That's because you like her, big time,' added Robbo.

'Get real! Watch the game, will ya,' said Specky, wanting to change the subject, as his cheeks blushed brightly.

All the way through the third quarter, Specky couldn't stop thinking about Christina, even though the match was turning out to be a sensational battle. By the end of the quarter, the score was even: 10.10.70 for Geelong and 9.16.70 for Collingwood.

Robbo and Danny had become so wrapped

up in the match that they had forgotten about teasing Specky. They argued over the game tactics that Collingwood should take to win. Specky felt it was a good time to leave them and return to the vicinity of the Barassi Bar. He somehow hoped he would bump into Christina.

As he waited and watched hordes of fans enter and leave the bar, Specky realised that he would be extremely lucky to see her again. Why would she want to come back down here, anyway? he thought.

'Hey, Speck! What are you doing?'

It was Danny's Uncle Joe, leaving the bar with more drinks and snacks in his hands.

'Um, nothing. I was stretching my legs,' answered Specky.

'Well, help me carry these back, will you?' Uncle Joe handed over some of the snacks to Specky, and they made their way back to their seats. Specky glanced over his shoulder — no Christina.

I'll just have to wait until I get back home on the computer again, he thought.

'Hey, Speck. The last quarter has started already. You missed seeing a fantastic goal by our sensational captain. Where did you go?' asked Danny.

Specky sat down beside his friends.

'He probably went looking for Christina again, ooooewww!' added Robbo, with a smirk.

Specky blushed, then turned his attention to the game without responding. Geelong had just kicked a goal!

'Hey, Speck, imagine if your father, you know, your biological father, is here somewhere in the crowd. Wouldn't that be so weird?' remarked Robbo. 'Didn't you think he could be a Cats supporter? 'Cause in the baby photo you're dressed up in all that Geelong gear.'

Specky stared blankly at his friends, then into the sea of supporters around him, especially the Cats barrackers. It hadn't even crossed his mind.

'Yeah, how bizarre would that be,' agreed Danny.

Specky hadn't heard Danny. He was now deep in thought and intensely checking out the Geelong supporters, wondering if his real dad was there. Would Specky recognise him?

He continued to daydream. Maybe his real dad was really happy that Geelong was slightly in front. Maybe he was also screaming at the umpires, like Danny's Uncle Joe. It could be that bloke there, he sort of looks like me, he thought.

Specky was so distracted by his daydreaming that he hadn't even noticed that Geelong had kicked another two quick goals. That was, until Danny and his family and the rest of the Collingwood fans began screaming their disappointment. They could all sense that Geelong was on a winning streak.

'C'mon, Pies! Don't do this to us! Don't lose it in the final quarter!' pleaded Danny's uncles. Their voices were hoarse and croaky from shouting for most of the afternoon. Unfortunately, their pleas weren't enough. Geelong was beginning to steamroll Collingwood.

When the Cats took a five-goal lead with an amazing snap shot from their rover, Specky couldn't help jumping up in the air to applaud them. Danny and his family all glared at Specky, shocked by his actions. Uncle Joe almost dropped his drink.

Danny pulled Specky back down to his seat. 'What are you doing? Don't tell me you barrack for Geelong now?' he asked, feeling slightly betrayed.

Specky wasn't sure how to answer Danny. He didn't know why he was suddenly happy for

Geelong — that is, until Robbo's next comment.

'I know why he likes the Cats now. It's 'cause of his father, the dad he hasn't met. He thinks if he was with him now, they'd both be barracking for Geelong. Isn't that right, Speck?'

Specky nodded. 'Yeah, that's it. You're right!'

'I can't believe you, Speck,' said Danny, shaking his head. 'You're the only person I know who barracks for *six* teams.'

'Well, I'm not sure if I want to barrack for them full-time, but even if I do, it isn't a crime, is it?' said Specky in his own defence.

Just then the final siren echoed throughout the stadium — the game was over. Geelong had defeated Collingwood by five goals.

Specky looked over to Danny's family — they all looked absolutely miserable. Uncle Joe was mumbling to himself, still blaming the umpires for the upsetting loss. Uncle Santo, his children and his friends Ron and Adrian all shuffled out of the stadium as fast as they could. They couldn't bear listening to the Geelong theme song blasting through the speakers — it was torture. As for Danny, his father and his younger brother Phillip, they looked as if someone had just died. And all the way home no one said a word.

'Thanks for taking me, Mr Castelino,' said Specky when they got to his house. 'See ya, Danny. See ya, Robbo. See you on Monday.'

And with that, Specky's extraordinary day at the MCG was over.

'So, how was it?' asked Specky's mother, as he entered the house.

'It was great,' Specky said in passing, on his way to the fridge. He grabbed a couple of cheese slices and joined his mother, who was sitting at the kitchen table organising the bills.

'Mum, I've been thinking. You know how you and Alice are good at maths? Well, do you think Alice got her talent for being good with figures from you?'

Specky's mum put down her pencil and looked up at Specky curiously. 'You mean inherited it from me?'

'Yeah, that's it!' said Specky.

'Well, I don't think so. Alice is good at maths because she does her homework and I'm here to help her out, not because she was born with mathematical talent!'

'But Alice has your eyes and the same straight reddish hair as you. So why wouldn't she have the same mathematical brain like you? Why couldn't she have been born with it?'

'Simon, I know where you're heading with this. Just because you're adopted, it doesn't mean that you should feel like you have missed out in any way. We've given you everything. We've given you a better life than what you would have had. Now please, honey, let me finish what I'm doing here.'

Specky's mum dropped her head back in to her work. It was obvious to Specky that she didn't want to look directly at him, as if she had said something that she shouldn't have. Specky was left to wonder for rest of the day what she meant by 'a better life than what you would have had.'

The following morning, Specky couldn't wait to get on the Internet. He really hoped he would be able to chat to Christina again. But unfortunately, she didn't log on for the entire day. Feeling a little down, Specky decided to read the pamphlets she had given him. He read about adopted adult children finding their long-lost biological parents. Some of the stories were very moving. Specky once again began fantasising about what it would be like to find his dad. What would he say to him? Hi. My name is Simon, but everyone calls me Specky. I'm your son! Specky chuckled to himself. But then he started feeling a little guilty. 'What am I doing? I have a father already. This is dumb!' he said under his breath. Thinking about all of this adoption stuff was really starting to get to him.

Specky tossed the pamphlets under his bed, determined to try to forget about it all. But it was no use. By the time Monday afternoon rolled around, Specky was back in his bedroom searching for them. When he finally found them, he ran into the study, slammed the door behind him, and picked up the phone. He nervously dialled the number at the bottom of one of the pamphlets. He took in a deep breath. His hands were shaking.

'Hello, Adoption Information Service, Marge speaking. Hello?'

Specky froze for a second. He couldn't believe what he was actually doing.

'Um, yes, hello . . .' Specky's voice wobbled. 'I'm calling 'cause I want to find my dad. He loves footy!'

17

DAD?

Specky knew that he had already gone too far. This was it. For a moment he considered hanging up, but instead he repeated what he had just said a few moments ago.

'Yes, I want to find my biological father. I know he loves footy, and he probably barracks for Geelong. Oh, I also know that my biological mother is dead. She was killed in a car accident. Well, that's what I was told ...'

Specky hadn't realised that he was rambling on. The female voice on the other end of the line stopped him mid-sentence.

'You sound kind of young. Can I ask how old are you?'

'I'm 12,' replied Specky.

'Hmm,' began the lady. 'Unfortunately, the

legal age to search for your biological parents in this state is 18, unless you have the consent of your adoptive parents.'

'Oh . . .' said a deflated Specky.

'Why don't you get your adoptive parents to call and we can arrange a time for you all to come in and chat?'

Specky hurriedly thanked the lady for her help, then dropped the phone. His search for his 'footy father' hadn't even got out of the starting blocks. Specky knew that his mum and dad would never consider such a thing — the way they acted the other night was proof of that. But suddenly Specky had an idea.

Maybe someone else could act as one of his parents. Specky smiled to himself. It was an outrageous plan, but worth a shot. He ran downstairs, out through the front door and all the way to Robbo's house.

'Well, I'm very flattered, Specky, I really am,' said Robbo's father. 'But I can't accept your offer. Even though I do sometimes feel that you're like another son to me . . . I mean, you're always around here. No, I think you should let your parents know how you're feeling. I'm sure they'll help you search for your biological dad — if that's what you really want.'

Specky shrugged his shoulders. He was disappointed that Robbo's father couldn't help, but he understood.

Later that evening he decided to take Robbo's dad's advice and approach his parents. It was after dinner, and they were all in the lounge room watching TV. 'Um, Mum, Dad, can I ask you something?'

Specky's parents hadn't heard him. They were engrossed in a movie. That was, until Specky said, 'It's about finding my biological father.'

Now he had their attention. Specky's dad abruptly switched the TV off. His mother was the first to respond.

'Simon, what did we tell you? *We're* your parents. There's nothing else you need to know.'

Specky could tell his mother was getting upset again. 'I know that, Mum, but isn't it my right to know? I mean, I know that other adopted kids have had the chance to find out.' Specky wasn't going to tell them that he had been doing some research.

'No, it's not your right!' snapped Specky's dad. 'You're much too young. Maybe when you're an adult you can have the right. But until then we're your parents! How many times do we have to tell you! Now go upstairs to your room out of my sight!'

Specky sat on his bed, thinking about what had just happened. He knew it was of no use now to ask his parents to join him in a visit to the adoption information office. He also knew that there was nothing else he could do. Specky thought his search for his 'footy father' was now over — or at least on hold for the next six years.

Or maybe not ...

The next day after school, Specky logged onto his computer. He was happy to see an instant message from Christina pop up on the screen:

CHRISkicks: It was nice meeting you the other day.

FOOTYHEAD: Thanks! It was cool meeting you, too!

Specky was unaware that his face had turned bright pink.

CHRISkicks: Hey, I'm glad you're online!

FOOTYHEAD: Why?

CHRISkicks: Have you read the *Herald Sun* today?

FOOTYHEAD: No.

CHRISkicks: I think you should.

FOOTYHEAD: Why?

CHRISkicks: Just go and read it — there's an article you should look at. The heading is 'HELLO, DADDY?' Read it and then call me. Here's my number . . .

Specky was definitely curious to find out what Christina was talking about. He was also excited that she had given him her number. He smiled at the thought of them becoming closer friends. He had never felt this way about a girl before.

Specky logged off and ran downstairs to look for the paper.

'Mum, where's today's newspaper?' he shouted.

'I didn't get it!' came her response from the kitchen.

Specky hurried to the milk bar at the end of his street. He picked up the newspaper and quickly flipped through the pages — there was the article. It read:

HELLO, DADDY?

Is former Geelong champion Blade 'Bazza' Furlington a father? Well, the AFL legend turned world champion kickboxer, part-time film actor and regular guest on Australia's number-one footy show, *Sensational Stuff!*, is accused of being many things — it comes with the role of being a high-profile celebrity. But could the former Geelong legend, and Australia's most eligible bachelor, also be a dad?

Well, Beverly Yam of Fernsville thinks so. The elderly woman claims that her daughter, who was killed in a car accident 10 years ago, once dated Furlington and gave birth to a boy before she passed away. The boy's father? Our beloved Bazza!

Ms Yam states that she wasn't on speaking terms with her daughter back then, and that the two-year-old baby boy was later adopted out by other family members. She claims that Furlington didn't want to take the child in, fearing it would damage his career and sex-symbol image. Ms Yam believes that somewhere out there is a 12-year-old boy who belongs back with her and that Furlington should financially support them both.

When approached by us, Furlington denied the claim as 'outlandish'. 'I get a dozen of these accusations a day from people wanting to make a quick buck,' he said.

Specky gasped. Could Blade Furlington, one of the most famous sporting figures in the country, be my father? he wondered.

18

BULLY PLAY

When Specky got back home he decided not to call Christina straight away. Instead, he wandered into his backyard and decided to toss a ball to Sammy a few times. So many thoughts were swirling around in his head.

Specky decided that it all made sense — he was dressed up in Geelong gear as a baby in that picture because his real dad played for Geelong. And the whole thing about Specky's biological mother being killed in a car accident. And the fact that he's good at footy. The pieces all fitted together. He must be Blade Furlington's son!

Specky wasn't sure how he should feel. Excited? Relieved? Both?

Eventually he went inside and called Christina.

'I can't believe it!' said Specky.

'That's what I thought. I remembered you telling me about the picture and your biological mum. When I first read the newspaper, I thought it sounded like the woman in the article had just made it up — but it's too much of a coincidence, don't you think?' asked Christina.

'I don't know what to think,' replied Specky.

Christina could sense that Specky was feeling overwhelmed.

'Hey, having Blade Furlington as your dad isn't such a bad thing, you know. You said you were hoping your biological dad was into footy — well, you can't get more of a footy father than Blade.'

Specky let out a nervous laugh. But his conversation with Christina was cut short because his sister entered the room.

'Can you get off the phone?' she ordered. 'I'm expecting an important call.' Alice stood over Specky, tapping her foot.

Specky whispered back into the phone. 'I'll talk to you later. Bye.'

As soon as Specky put the phone down Alice started interrogating him.

'What was all that about?' she asked.

'Nothing,' replied Specky.

'Yeah, sure. Who were you talking to on the phone? You're hiding something, aren't you?'

Specky was a terrible liar, but there was no way he was going to let his sister in on what he had just been talking about.

When it came to Robbo and Danny, though, that was another story. The three boys were walking home from school the next day when Specky spilled the beans.

'No way! That's so cool! You'll be able to get us tickets to see *Sensational Stuff!*. He's always on the show,' said Danny.

'Now you'll *have* to barrack for Geelong! Are you sure he's your dad?' added Robbo.

'No, I'm not exactly sure, but everything points towards it being true. Blade just hasn't admitted it yet. I sort of have his nose, don't you think?'

'What are you going to do now?' asked Danny.

'I don't know. I was thinking I'd write him a letter. I'm not sure if I want to meet the old woman from Fernsville — the one who spoke to the newspapers.'

'You know that *woman* is your grandmother,' said Robbo.

Specky hadn't made the connection until that very moment. He was so caught up with his new-found 'celebrity dad' that he hadn't thought about the rest of his biological family.

'Hey, look. I wonder what they want?' said Danny.

Specky looked up to see that three other boys, a couple of years older than him, were approaching him and his friends.

'Is that your footy?' one of them asked, pointing at the Sherrin football Robbo was holding under his arm.

'Yes,' said Robbo, looking slightly worried.

'Well, I don't think so. It looks like mine,' grumbled the other boy.

Specky could sense that there was trouble brewing. 'Just ignore them, Robbo. Let's keep walking,' he said.

'You're not going anywhere until you give it to me!'

The older boys stood directly in front of Specky, Danny and Robbo, and blocked them from passing.

'Get lost, will ya! Go and pick on someone your own size,' yelled Danny.

'Oooh, tough words, shrimp,' cackled the tallest of the bullies as he suddenly lunged towards Robbo and snatched the younger boy's football.

'Creep! Thief!' said Robbo, as he watched the bully run off with the ball and casually kick it around with his mates.

Specky and Danny also looked on, stunned.

'We've got to get it back. It was a gift from my dad,' said Robbo.

'They'll kill us! Look how big they are,' said Danny, who was now having second thoughts about standing up to the older kids.

'Well, we can't let them steal Robbo's footy, that's for sure,' said Specky. 'Let's go for it.'

Specky dropped his school bag and charged for the bullies. Danny and Robbo hesitantly ran after him.

The bullies sniggered to themselves as they watched Specky charge for them. 'Come and get it! Come on, here it is,' they teased.

They were happy to play and torment Specky and his friends. Every time Robbo, Danny or Specky got close to the football, the older boys quickly kicked it away. They out-marked, outran and out-dodged Specky and his friends. Robbo and Danny were becoming visibly frustrated, and more upset with each missed grab. As for Specky, he was determined to keep his cool.

Then one of the bullies kicked a wobbly old punt.

'This is it,' whispered Specky under his breath, 'it's mine.'

He made a dash towards the ball as it began its slow descent.

The bully nervously positioned himself underneath it. He knew he had messed up the kick. His mates were screaming at him to hurry.

Specky grinned. He knew this was his chance. He imagined he was playing in the grand final, and the team's success depended on this crucial mark!

'It's mine,' he continued to say to himself, as he drew in closer to the bully.

The bully stumbled back and forth, trying not to lose sight of ball or to be put off by Specky's fast advance.

'Time to fly!' shouted Specky at the top of his lungs.

Danny and Robbo stopped running and looked on as their friend took an almighty leap for the sky. Their jaws dropped in unison. They were witnessing the biggest spring Specky had ever made. Not even during their Saturday morning matches had they seen him get up so high before.

'Yahooooo! Go Speck! Unreal!!!' they yelled proudly.

Specky hadn't taken his eye off the ball. He gracefully soared a metre above the bully's shoulders, digging his shoes into the bully's face on the way. With his fingers fully extended he lunged for the ball, and successfully grabbed hold of it. It was a sensational specky!

The other bullies watched on, shocked, as Specky landed firmly on both feet. They shook their heads, completely taken aback by his talent.

'I don't believe it,' one of them gasped.

'Get him!' shouted the leader.

'Go, Speck! GO!' hollered Robbo and Danny, as they grabbed all of their school bags and scurried off in the opposite direction.

Specky ran as he had never run before. He didn't dare look back, but he could sense that the bullies were in hot pursuit. His lungs were burning and his heart pounded loudly against his ribcage. It was difficult to sprint with a footy in one hand, but he wasn't going to let that get in the way. Specky bolted across the park, then threw himself over a fence, shot off down an alleyway, sprinted through a stranger's back yard, charged up over a steep hill, then darted across a bridge, and finally made it into his street. He choked for air as he slowed down to an exhausted and unstable jog. His face was dripping with perspiration.

When Specky reached his house he collapsed in a heap on the front lawn. Panting and puffing, he just managed to raise his head to make sure that the bullies were nowhere in sight. He had successfully escaped from them — with Robbo's ball safely in hand.

But just as he thought he had had enough drama for one afternoon, his mother called him in to pick up the phone. He stumbled back to his feet and wobbled into the house to take the call. It was Christina on the other end.

'Hi Specky. My dad is directing tomorrow night's live show of *Sensational Stuff!* and told me that Blade Furlington will be a guest on it. Would you like to come with me and see the show? I thought it might cheer you up, and you'll be able to get a closer look at your real dad. We may even be able to meet him after the telecast. So, how about it?'

19

CHRISTINA'S CARLTON

'Specky, are you there?'

Christina could hear Specky gasp. She could tell he was shocked by her generous invitation.

'Yeah, I'm here,' he replied, still panting heavily from his terrifying run.

'Well, what do you think? We can pick you up after school. You can have dinner at my place, then we'll go with Dad to the TV studios. Okay?'

Specky paused before giving an answer. A million questions ran through his head. What was he doing? How could he do this to his mum and dad? But what if Blade was his father? Would he go to watch Specky play footy? That would be the best. Maybe they could just be friends? But would that be right?

Would Specky live with him? But he didn't really want to leave Mum, Dad and Alice. Maybe he could arrange visits to Blade's home? Maybe Specky could have two dads? Maybe this was his only chance? Specky wondered what Blade was like in real life. Would he be like Specky? What did he have to lose?'

Specky let out a big sigh.

'Yes, I'll come,' he said hastily. They then made plans about where to meet.

'Bye, Specky. And don't worry, it's going to be so much fun.'

'Yeah, okay, bye,' said Specky, hanging up the phone, not convinced that he had made the right decision.

Later that evening, in bed, he tossed and turned, thinking about the big day that awaited him. He finally got to sleep around 3.00 a.m. At breakfast he realised he would have to explain to his mother that he wouldn't be around after school.

'Mum, Robbo asked me over to his house after school today. I'm invited for dinner. We're going to work on our homework together. Will that be okay?'

'Sure. But let Robbo's parents know I want you back at a reasonable hour.'

Specky caught Alice glaring at him suspiciously from across the table, and he started to feel a little uneasy about lying to his mother.

'Sure. See ya, Mum,' he said as he rushed out of the house.

Once at school, Specky found it difficult not to say anything to his friends about his big night. But he held his tongue. He was nervous enough, and letting his friends know would make him even more edgy. So he was glad that there were other things to distract him — like Robbo's and Danny's black eyes!

'You mean those guys stopped chasing me and then went after you? No wonder I got away from them so easily,' said Specky. He took a closer look at the shiners that his friends had been given by the bullies. They appeared somewhat proud of their bruises.

'Yeah, they couldn't believe you got the ball. It was like, the best mark I've ever seen. I mean, just the best. They should sing "Up there Specky" instead of "Up there Cazaly"!' said Danny.

'Thanks, Speck. So where is it?' asked Robbo as he handed Specky's school bag back to him.

'Oh, man. Robbo, I totally forgot it. Sorry. Just come over and pick it up whenever you want — but not today. Actually, can you cover

137

for me after school? I told my mum I'm having dinner at your place tonight.'

'Why did you say that?'

'I bet it's got something to do with Blade Furlington, hasn't it?' suggested Danny.

'Um, look, I can't say. Can you do it for me, Robbo?'

Robbo reluctantly nodded, slightly disappointed that his best mate was hiding something from him.

For the rest of the day, Specky tried to concentrate on his schoolwork, but he found it extremely difficult. Instead of focusing on Maths, Geography, English, even kick-to-kick with his classmates during recess, all he could think about was the show. Eventually the final bell of the day sounded and Specky made his way to the front of the school to wait for Christina as planned.

'Come on, Speck. What are you doing?'

Specky turned to see that Danny and Robbo were waving him to join them.

'Speck, have you forgotten? We have footy training.'

Specky winced. For the first time ever, he had totally forgotten. Footy had always come first — but not today.

'I'm not coming,' he announced.

Danny and Robbo almost fell over backwards in disbelief. 'What do you mean, you're not coming? You always come.'

Specky just stared at his mates, and forced himself not to say a word.

'Well, whatever you're doing, Speck, it must be important for you to miss training, so good luck,' said Robbo.

'Good luck? That's it? Specky is missing training for the first time ever and you don't want to know why?' said Danny, gently slapping Robbo. 'Well, *I* do. Specky, tell us, what are you up to?'

'I can't say, okay? I'll tell you later. Can you tell the Coach I was feeling sick or something?' Specky looked the other way. He forced himself not to give in to Danny's persistence.

'Come on. Let's go,' said Robbo, tugging at Danny's jumper. 'He'll tell us when he wants to. See ya, Speck.'

Danny groaned and complained, but headed off with Robbo to training.

Specky glanced back at his friends. He wanted so much to chase after them. He was beginning to have doubts.

'Maybe I shouldn't go,' he muttered.

Just then, a shiny brand-new black BMW pulled up directly beside him. It was Christina and her dad.

'Dad, this is Specky,' said Christina. She grinned at Specky as he hopped into the back seat.

'Pleasure to meet you, Specky. Christina told me that you're just as mad for footy as she is and that I had to let you both come to the show tonight. I understand that you two have become very good friends . . .'

Specky glanced over to Christina, who continued to look back from the front passenger seat smiling at him.

'But I have to say,' added Christina's father, 'when I found out that my daughter met you over the Internet, well — it's simply something I don't condone. And she should have known better. What do your parents think about this?'

'Um, well, um,' Specky gulped, unprepared for the question. 'Um, they're fine with it,' he lied nervously.

'Hmm? Well, she knows I'm not happy with her at the moment. Don't you?'

'Dad!' Christina felt slightly embarrassed about being reprimanded in front of Specky again. Specky gave her a smirk.

When Christina's dad drove into the driveway of their home in Carlton, Christina couldn't wait to rush Specky inside. She hurriedly introduced him to her mother, then dragged him into her bedroom to show him her collection of footy memorabilia.

'Wow!' gasped Specky. 'It's like an AFL shrine in here.' Specky stared in awe at the personally autographed photos of past and present AFL champions hanging from the walls.

'Yeah, that's the good thing about having a dad involved in sports television,' said Christina proudly. 'So, how are you feeling about tonight?' she asked.

'Um, really nervous. No one knows I'm here. I should be at footy training.'

'Well, like I said, don't worry, we'll have fun.'

Specky sighed, still staring up at the famous photographs.

Christina could sense that he was feeling a little uncomfortable, so she invited him to join her in the backyard. She grabbed her football on the way out.

'Okay, show me your stuff,' she said, hand-balling the footy to Specky.

Specky grinned as Christina ran back a few metres. 'My stuff?'

'Yeah, let's kick the ball around. Girls can play too, you know.'

Specky blushed. Although he had never played footy with a girl, he felt at ease once he kicked a short floating punt to Christina. They then continued to kick the ball to each other for the next half an hour or so.

'You're not bad,' teased Christina.

'Well, you're pretty good yourself,' said Specky, impressed.

The two paused for a second and smiled.

'Well, we'd better go in and have dinner. It'll be time to go soon.'

They made their way inside and sat down to have an early dinner. Christina's mother had put on a lavish meal, but unfortunately Specky couldn't eat much. His stomach was full of butterflies, especially after Christina's father said in passing, 'Well, we're expecting big ratings again tonight, especially having Blade as guest. Last week we had over 700,000 viewers. The camera always pans over the studio audience. If you're lucky you might get your face on TV tonight, Specky!'

Specky let out a nervous chuckle, and before he knew it, he, Christina and her father were on their way to the TV studios. As they drove through the gates and into the parking lot, Specky began nervously biting his fingernails. This was it. He was finally going to get a real life look at his real father.

20

FOOTY FAME

Once inside the TV studio, Christina's father darted off to join the camera crew and prepare for the broadcast. As for Christina and Specky, they were greeted by the segment producer of the show.

'Hi, Christina. Nice to see you again.'

'Hi, Jen,' replied Christina.

'So, this must be Specky Magee. Hi, Specky,' said the friendly lady, who leaned forward to shake Specky's hand.

Specky responded with a shy 'Hi'. He had to pinch himself. He still couldn't actually believe he was here.

'Okay, well, follow me, guys. I'm going to take you to where you'll be sitting during the show.'

Christina winked at Specky as they followed Jen down one of the many long corridors that led into the large warehouse-like studio.

'We're expecting a great show tonight!' she added. 'Now, Christina, your dad mentioned something about you and Specky hoping to meet Blade Furlington after the show. Well, as I told him, I can't promise anything. Blade's a busy man and he may have to rush out after his appearance, but leave it to me, I'll see what I can do.'

'Thanks,' said Christina. She then turned to Specky — he was doing his best to contain his excitement.

'Well, here it is,' said Jen as she led Specky and Christina into the main studio of the building.

Specky's entire face lit up. Lights hung from the tall ceilings and large cameras stood motionless around the set like sleeping robots from some sci-fi film. 'Oh man, I can't believe I'm on the set of *Sensational Stuff!*,' he whispered.

Jen left Specky and Christina to take their seats. All they had to do now was wait. Within minutes, an excited crowd of people flowed into the studio. They were the studio audience for the night. Many had waited weeks, even months, to get tickets to the popular football show.

Specky took in a deep breath. Christina gently nudged him.

'Not long before you'll be only metres away from him. Are you okay?'

Specky nodded nervously, unaware that he was biting his bottom lip. His heart was racing and his palms felt wet and clammy.

There was a real buzz of anticipation from the studio crowd as the beginning of the show drew nearer. Most of them were proudly wearing their club colours, ready to cheer and scream when the host of the show, Teddy McMahon, mentioned their team.

Finally, the moment had come. Kevin Jam, the show's comedian, walked onto the set and the audience started applauding.

'He's come in to warm up the crowd — get them all excited,' whispered Christina into Specky's ear.

'*More* excited? They look pretty pumped up to me,' replied Specky, as he watched Kevin tell a few jokes and introduce the guest footballers. 'Oh my God, it's the captain of Collingwood, Hawthorn's star full-forward and Melbourne's ruckman ...' Specky gasped as he watched the players seat themselves behind a specially made desk positioned at the front of the stage.

'Okay, everyone!' shouted the floor manager. 'It's showtime! Three, two, one ...'

Suddenly the show's theme music echoed throughout the studio, as opening credits and images aired across tens of thousands of television screens nationwide. The studio audience, including Specky and Christina, applauded as Teddy McMahon made his entrance.

'Good evening and welcome to *Sensational Stuff!*,' he announced enthusiastically. 'What a show we have for you tonight. And as usual, we've seen some sensational stuff all this week in footy.'

There was another cheer from the audience. 'We're going to tackle the big issue of a certain club president who was caught wearing pyjamas featuring another team's colours this week, and we'll also look at the difficulties experienced by female players who want to enter the AFL, and much, much more. But for now, let me introduce our guest players ...' Again, more cheers.

'And finally, a man who is never out of the news. Put your hands together for my co-host and number one sidekick, Mr Johnny Parker.'

Specky applauded along with everyone else. He was trying really hard to enjoy the show, but he was still so nervous. For the next few minutes everything seemed like one big daze. Specky kept asking himself what he was doing there. He watched on blankly as Teddy and Johnny performed their usual showbiz banter. Then, taking Specky by complete surprise, Teddy introduced their special guest — Blade Furlington!

Specky froze in his seat. He had seen Blade on TV so many times before, but this time everything would be totally different. Instead of watching a celebrity at work, tonight he was watching his very own father!

Blade received a rousing reception from the studio audience when he walked onto the stage. He took a seat next to Johnny Parker, and the interview began.

'So, Blade,' began Johnny, with a cheeky smirk, 'usually *I'm* the one hogging the headlines, but this week you've outdone me, mate. We understand that you became an instant father this week.'

There was a ripple of laughter from everyone in the audience — except for Specky. He took in a deep breath, sensing Blade's stare would turn on him soon.

'Well, Johnny, as you know, if I listened to all of the crazy claims people make to earn a few dollars, I'd be the father of one hundred kids by now!'

Again the audience laughed.

'Well, the woman who came out and made this statement is supposedly pretty convincing. She says that there's a 12-year-old boy out there who is *your* son. What have you got to say about that, Blade?'

'I know, Johnny, it sounds convincing but there's no way I have a son!'

Christina gently nudged Specky in response to Blade's last comment. But Specky was so focused on Blade that he didn't even notice her do it.

'Well, mate, let's see what some of the audience members have to say,' said Johnny, suddenly getting up out of his chair and making his way over to the studio crowd. Like an American talkshow host, Johnny, now holding a hand-held microphone, approached a woman wearing a Demons scarf. She was sitting only a metre or so away from where Specky and Christina were seated. 'So, madam, what's your opinion of all of this?' Johnny shoved the mike close to her face.

'Well, Johnny, he can have my kids any day! You're absolutely gorgeous, Blade!'

The audience laughed while back on stage Blade blushed.

'And you, sir?' Johnny leant over to an elderly man kitted out in Richmond colours, seated next to the woman.

'I think it's a disgrace!' he said in a more serious tone. He then turned his stare on Blade. 'Young man, I think you should grow up and take responsibility now that you're a father!'

'But he's not a father! It was just a claim!' added Johnny.

'Well, he should stop living the high life. Dads don't do that!' The old man had missed the point, and there were scattered giggles throughout the studio.

'Sir, no disrespect intended, but let me say this again very slowly,' said Johnny, now playing up to the crowd. 'Blade Furlington is not a father!'

'Yes he is!' blurted Christina.

'Excuse me?' said Johnny.

Specky's jaw dropped. He turned to Christina and gave her a look as if to say 'What do you think you're doing?' Christina sank back into her seat, regretting what she had just done. She hadn't intended anyone to hear her. But it was too late. Johnny was now standing above her.

'So what did you say, young lady?' he asked. Johnny lowered his microphone right between Specky and Christina. Specky dropped his head, too embarrassed to look up. Johnny hadn't recognised Christina as the daughter of the show's director.

'Um ...' Christina nervously began to say. 'Yes, he is a father!'

'And why do you say that?' asked Johnny.

'Because this is his son,' said Christina, gesturing to Specky. Some of the audience gasped.

'And who are you?' said Johnny, turning towards Specky.

Specky slowly raised his head to Johnny. He couldn't believe this was happening. He felt his heart was in his throat. 'My name is Specky Magee,' he said softly.

Danny and Robbo were both watching *Sensational Stuff!* at home with their families, and they almost had a fit when they saw their friend on TV.

'Oh my God! It's Specky! It's Specky!' screamed Danny, jumping up and down on the spot.

'Dad, Dad! Look at this! It's Specky on the telly!' shouted Robbo, turning up the volume. 'So that's what he was hiding!'

Over at Specky's house, Alice had just a received a call from one of her school friends.

'Alice, your brother is on TV!'

Alice rushed into the lounge room, called in her parents and switched on the TV.

'So, Specky,' continued Johnny, 'what makes you think that Blade here could be your father?'

Specky let out a nervous cough and cleared his throat. 'Um, well I was told by my parents ...'

'Your adoptive parents,' Teddy interjected from behind the desk on stage.

'Yeah, my parents told me that all they knew when they got me as a baby from the adoption agency is that my biological mother was killed in a car accident, just like the woman in the newspaper said. And I also found a photo of myself when I was a couple of years old, dressed up in Geelong gear!'

Johnny turned towards Blade. 'Well, Blade, or should I say, Dad, what do you think of that?'

The audience sniggered as Blade let out a nervous laugh. It was obvious to everyone that he was caught totally off-guard and was taken aback. He paused for what seemed an eternity before speaking.

'Johnny, Teddy, if I can just say a few words to young Specky?'

The two hosts gestured for Blade to continue. He then turned towards Specky. 'Specky, I'm guessing you're pretty good at footy with a name like that?'

Specky blushed and nodded.

'And you come across as a well-mannered, intelligent kid. They are all attributes any father would be proud of. I'm also guessing that your adoptive parents love you very much, and they've done a good job raising you so far, right?'

Specky nodded again.

'What are you trying to say, Blade?' interrupted Johnny.

'The point I'm trying to make is that I'm very flattered to think a great kid like Specky would even consider me as his father, but I'm sorry to say I'm not his dad. Just over an hour ago the woman who made the claim confessed to the police that she had made up the entire story. I guess I should have mentioned that before Johnny approached the audience. So Specky, I'm very sorry. I'm not your father, and I do hope you'll find him one day. But if I can offer some advice, I think you should be happy with your adoptive parents. It appears to me that they've done a fantastic job raising you. You seem like a good kid.'

The audience could tell that the high-profile, usually outspoken celebrity was being very sincere. They all applauded him.

As for Specky, he tried to smile and not look too upset.

Back at his home, Specky's stunned mother switched off the TV and turned to her husband. 'He was meant to be at Robbo's.' Her eyes were teary. 'This has gone too far. We have to tell him the truth!'

21

THE TRUTH

By the time the last audience member had left, the make-up had been scrubbed off Teddy's and Johnny's faces, and the final studio lights had been switched off, it was after midnight. Christina and her father dropped Specky off back at his house, and he sadly trudged across the front lawn of his home, knowing it was an evening he would never forget. He quietly opened the front door, only to discover that his parents were waiting for him in the lounge room — 'I'm sorry I'm so late, Robbo and I lost track of the time. Robbo's parents said that they are very sorry about . . .'

'Simon, stop! We know. We saw you on TV, now sit down,' instructed Specky's dad.

Specky stared down at his feet, too embarrassed to look directly into his father's eyes, and slumped onto the couch.

'Simon, it's time for us to tell you the truth about your biological parents.'

'The truth?' said Specky softly, raising his head.

Specky's father took in a deep breath. 'Yes, we haven't been exactly honest with you. We felt we'd never really have to tell you — not at your age, anyway. The way you conducted yourself on that show tonight, well, we're proud of you.'

Specky was surprised.

'Proud of me?' he said softly.

'Yes, proud,' added Specky's mother. 'You were very mature in the way you acted. Mind you, I was upset to see you there on TV, and to find out you had lied to me. But under the circumstances . . .'

'What your mother and I are trying to say is that we'll tell you everything. We were fooling ourselves to think this day would never come. We realise now that we were only thinking of ourselves, protecting our own insecurities, so here goes . . .' Specky's father gently squeezed his wife's hand. 'Your biological father is . . .'

Specky's father took another breath. 'Your biological father is my brother Bob!'

Specky was shocked, and the news took a few seconds to sink in.

'Your brother Bob? You mean Uncle Bob? The uncle that Alice and I have never met? The brother you don't keep in touch with and have nothing to do with?'

Specky's parents glanced at each other and nodded. Specky was stunned. He didn't know what to say next, except, 'How? Why?'

This time Specky's mum spoke. 'Your biological parents are Bob and his girlfriend at the time, Lisa. Sadly Lisa was involved in a terrible car accident and unfortunately she died, leaving Bob to look after you. Your Uncle Bob was so devastated by Lisa's death that he couldn't cope with raising a baby by himself. He was a mess. He didn't have a job — he was an unemployed actor waiting for his big break. He begged us to take you in while he tried to get his life together. As we looked after you, days turned into months, and we urged Bob to get a job, find a place to live, and take you back and be a responsible father. But unfortunately, Bob decided he just couldn't do that. So he packed all his possessions and told us he was leaving to go and live up in Sydney and that he wanted us to be your legal parents for good. We were so appalled by his actions — leaving his own child behind — that we agreed, but knew that it was unlikely we'd ever have much to do with him again. That was, until now. Since you discovered that photo. But saying that, Simon, we also wanted a little boy, and we were so happy to have you come into our lives.'

Specky sank back into the couch and let out a huge sigh. He watched his mother wipe away the tears she had streaming down her cheeks.

'We can get in contact with him, if you want,' added Specky's father.

Specky began to cry.

His mouth was dry and he felt all choked up. It was hard to say anything, so he just nodded.

'Fine, I'll call him tomorrow. Now it's time for bed,' said Specky's dad.'

The following morning, everyone in Specky's household was running late. It had been an emotional night to say the least, and no one had slept very well. Specky rushed to school, feeling confused and unsure about what he had found out the night before. But as soon as he got to the school building he discovered that he was now a celebrity among his classmates, so he had no time to think about Uncle Bob.

'Specky, we saw you last night. Why didn't you tell us?' shouted Danny, as he and Robbo rushed up to him.

All the students in Specky's class surrounded him, desperate to learn more about his TV appearance. Some students even asked for Specky's autograph. Specky couldn't believe the attention he was getting. Even a few of the teachers approached him during the day.

There was no escaping the constant fuss, not even on the footy ground the following Saturday morning. Specky took up his usual full-forward position, and the opposition's full-back couldn't stop staring at him for most of the game.

'That's where I've seen you!' he blurted out, while the ball was up the other end of the oval, and he and Specky were casually pacing in the goal square waiting for it to come down their way. 'You were on *Sensational Stuff!*. You thought Blade Furlington was your father.' The full-back sniggered to himself.

Specky did his best to ignore him, and tried to focus his attention on the play ahead of him.

'I can't wait to tell my family about this! I played against a famous person!'

Specky rolled his eyes. He couldn't understand why it was such a big deal to so many people. All he knew was that he wanted things to get back to normal — even with the knowledge that Uncle Bob was his real father. He glanced over to the boundary line to see the fathers of all his team-mates cheering the team on as usual.

It would be pretty cool to have Uncle Bob here watching me play, thought Specky.

The game ended with Specky's team winning once again. Specky was glad to be in Robbo's father's car and heading back home, away from all the gawking and unsettling attention.

'So, Speck, what happens now in terms of you finding your biological father? Will you wait a few years, until you're a little older?' asked Robbo's dad, staring back at Specky from the rear-view mirror.

With all the weird things that had been happening over the last few days, Specky hadn't told anyone, not even Robbo and Danny, about Uncle Bob.

'Um, my parents told me who he was after the TV show,' answered Specky, as if it was no big deal.

'Really? Who is it?' asked Robbo.

'It's a long story,' said Specky, aware that they had pulled up alongside his house.

'We understand,' added Robbo's father. 'You can fill us in when you're ready, mate. Great game today. Bye, Speck!'

Specky hopped out of the car and headed up the path to the front door of his house. He hadn't even noticed that there was an old white Kombi van parked in his parents' driveway.

As he opened the door, he was startled to see a stranger standing in the doorway.

'Hello, Simon?' the man asked.

Specky nodded, slightly startled. He knew straight away who this man standing in front of him was.

'I'm Bob — your dad. Nice to meet you.'

22

BOB

Specky abruptly dropped his sports bag on the floor. He looked around to see if his parents or Alice were nearby.

'They've gone out for the rest of the day, to let us get to know each other. I hope you don't mind. I have to say I was a little shocked to have got a call from my brother, telling me that he had told you everything.'

Specky wasn't sure what to say. He just stared at this tall, strange man, who looked like a hippy, left over from the '70s. He had long tangled hair and wore a loose cheesecloth shirt, leather-strapped beads, a multi-coloured vest, hessian-like pants and sandals.

'So you've been playing footy this morning.

That's cool. What position do you play?' he asked.

'Full-forward,' answered Specky.

'Cool!'

Specky could tell that Uncle Bob was just as nervous as he was. He also hadn't heard anyone who looked that old say 'cool' before.

'So,' Uncle Bob continued, 'I bet you kick a lot of goals. Um, have you eaten lunch? Would you like to?'

Specky nodded.

'Is Macca's okay with you? I love their French fries. I shouldn't, really. I usually only eat organic food — well, mostly. My girlfriend Becky would freak, but since it's a special occasion, why not!'

Specky nodded again and smiled — he loved fries from MacDonald's as well.

On the way there, both Specky and Bob began to relax with each other. Eventually they were talking nonstop.

'Yes, Becky and I have been together for three years now. We run a yoga centre and are also experimenting with a part-time retreat for stressed birds at the base of the Blue Mountains in New South Wales. We're real nature people.'

'Stressed birds?' asked Specky, curious to know more.

'Yeah, stressed pet birds like parrots and budgerigars. City owners and their birds come out to get away from it all. We let the birds fly freely, take in the fresh air. Get away from their stuffy cages.'

'But don't they fly away for good and not come back?'

'Well, yes, sometimes, but we let our clients know that if they fly away for good, it was meant to be. If they come back to them, then it's true love.'

'How many come back?'

'Well, none have flown back to their owners to date, but I'm sure there'll be some in the future that will.'

Specky tried not to giggle and appear impolite.

'And you make money from that?' he asked.

'No, like I said, we're experimenting. Thankfully we earn from the yoga centre, which Becky mainly runs. I'm an actor. I'm not sure if you were told that. My big break is just around the corner, I can feel it. I've just acted in a pilot for a new sitcom and I'm hoping to get a call any day now from my agent, saying a TV network has picked it up.'

Specky nodded, not sure about all the show business jargon, but slightly impressed nevertheless.

'Well, here we are,' said Bob, as he pulled up into a MacDonald's car park.

As they ordered their food and sat down at one of the vacant booths, Specky couldn't help thinking that Bob was definitely not the kind of footy dad he had imagined. He wondered if Bob still enjoyed Aussie Rules. 'Do you still barrack for Geelong?' asked Specky as he was about to take a bite from his McChicken burger.

'The footy team?'

Specky explained how he found the photograph of him dressed up in all the Geelong footy attire.

'I remember that! It was Lisa . . .' Bob paused for a second, as he realised just who he was talking to. 'Your mother. She was a die-hard Cats supporter. She was from Geelong. We met at an audition for a musical.'

'So do you still like footy?' asked a hopeful Specky.

'Yes, I do. But I don't follow it as much as I would like to. Becky's not into it. Actually, Lisa would have been proud to know that her son loved his footy. I'm kind of proud also, even though I haven't been a part of your life.'

There was another pause. Specky blushed, feeling slightly awkward.

'I would love to see you play. If that would be okay?'

Specky's face beamed. 'Sure. That would be great. I'm playing next Saturday. How long are you staying for?'

'A week, if that's okay with you. I'm staying in a nearby hotel. I don't want to make it uncomfortable for everyone at your place, if you know what I mean.'

For the following week, Specky and Bob made arrangements to see each other as often as they could. One afternoon, after school, Bob decided he would take Specky to the movies.

'Come in, Bob, let me get my jacket,' said Specky as he rushed upstairs to get it.

As Bob was left waiting in the hallway of the house he could see Specky's mum preparing dinner in the kitchen.

'Hi,' he said politely.

Specky's mum coolly said hi back. Bob felt a little uncomfortable, but he took a few steps closer and entered the kitchen.

166

'Um, Jane, I've been meaning to thank you,' he said.

'For what?' Specky's mum was chopping up some carrots. She didn't look up at Bob.

'For keeping me informed about Simon's life over the years. All those photos of him you sent me. His report cards, even his finger paintings. Well, I want to thank you for that.'

Specky's mum stopped chopping and turned to Bob. 'You're thanking the wrong person.'

'What?' asked Bob, looking surprised.

'You should be thanking your brother, not me. He sent all that stuff. If I'd my way, Bob, you wouldn't have got a single thing. Not only does your brother — my loving husband — constantly think about you, but he has been a wonderful father to Simon. I suppose you want him back now? Do you? Is that what you want, Bob?'

Bob was a little taken aback by Specky's mum confronting him.

'Well,' he began to say, 'I was thinking ...'

Just then Specky came bouncing in, wearing his jacket. 'So, are we ready?' he asked, unaware that he had interrupted a tense moment.

* * *

Later that evening, Bob and Specky were seated in the cinema. The movie had just started, when Bob's mobile started to ring.

Specky was embarrassed when everyone around them shushed Bob at the same time. But Bob still took his call, whispering loudly to the person on the other end. After hanging up, he leant towards Specky and said, 'That was an old friend of mine who lives here in Melbourne. He's now a film producer. Isn't that great? Anyway, he wanted to know if I could catch up with him in the next hour. I'm going to duck off and have a quick drink with him. I'll come back and get you after the movie.'

'But, didn't you want to watch this with me?'

'Sorry, mate. This is kind of important. I may get work out of this. You understand, don't you? I'll be back by the . . .'

Bob's mobile rang again and once more everyone in the cinema let out an annoyed, 'Shhhh!'

'That was him again. He's decided to cancel, something's come up. So now I'm staying!'

Bob looked back up at the screen and continued to watch the movie as if nothing had happened. For the rest of the film, Specky felt annoyed that Bob would have taken off and left him to watch the movie by himself.

But by the following day this was all soon forgotten, as both of them spent a couple of fun hours bike riding along the Yarra.

23

SENSITIVITY

It was Friday night before Specky had some time to himself. He was kicking his soft football toy around his bedroom when he suddenly heard a voice.

'Hey, squirt.' It was Alice, barging in again, without knocking. 'Are you having a good time with Bob?'

'Yeah, I am.'

'Are you going to move to his house in Sydney?'

Specky wasn't sure what to say. During the week he had fantasised about what it would be like to have Bob around full-time. He could definitely picture Bob coming to his footy games, and that's what he had wanted all along. But he hadn't really thought about living away from where he was now.

'I don't know,' he replied, shrugging his shoulders.

'Well, I know that Mum and Dad are freaking out about it. It's eating them up inside. I know their biggest fear is that they'll lose you,' added Alice.

Specky's stomach sank. He realised that his parents, especially his dad, had made a special effort to keep out of the way during Bob's visit. Until now, he hadn't thought about how they were feeling.

'And I'd have no one to pick on anymore if you moved away,' said Alice as she left the room.

Specky was touched by his sister's attempt to show him her true feelings. He took a deep breath and felt his heart skip a beat.

The following morning Specky was standing alongside his team-mates, ready to run out and play footy. He hadn't stopped smiling since he had woken up a few hours earlier. Bob had picked him up as planned, and had driven him to the game.

'Coach, this is ...' Specky paused for a moment, wondering how he was going to introduce Bob. 'This is ... my father, Bob.' Specky smiled, looking up back at Bob proudly. Bob blushed as Coach Pappas looked slightly confused. 'Your *dad?*' he asked. 'But I thought that ...'

'He's my biological father,' explained Specky.

'Oh, okay. Well, welcome. This team is very lucky to have someone like Specky,' said Coach Pappas, shaking Bob's hand.

Specky then introduced Bob to Danny and Robbo and the rest of the team. He was so happy to have someone there to watch him play. But not just anyone — his very own dad, like everyone else. This is what he had dreamt of for so long.

Specky ran to his position, joining his opponent from the other team. The umpire held the ball above his head and blew the whistle to signal the beginning of the game. Specky glanced over to the boundary line to see Bob standing with the other dads, smiling. Specky waved back at him. He was ready to play his best game ever.

24

FOREVER FATHER

Specky paced the goal square, eager for the ball to come his way. Unfortunately, the other team had got off to a superb start, and had taken Specky's team by surprise. In fact, the ball had only come down to Specky's end once, and even then he struggled to get a hand on it.

This wasn't the type of play he wanted Bob to see, and by the time the first-quarter whistle sounded, Coach Pappas wasn't the only one who was disappointed. Specky's team huddled together and faced their upset coach.

'I want you all to wake up!' he said, raising his voice. 'They've kicked four goals two to our big fat nothing. C'mon, guys! Snap out of it. I know you can play better than this.'

Specky hadn't heard his coach's plea. He was looking over at Bob, who had wandered away from the boundary line to talk on his mobile phone. Specky tried to get his attention, hoping he would look up, but he didn't. The umpire blew his whistle — it was the second quarter. Specky continued to look back at Bob as he ran to take up his position at the other goal square. He was still engrossed in his phone call, as he had been at the movies the other day.

'Specky!'

Specky looked up to see that the ball was heading his way. Danny broke away from the centre and stab-passed the ball to Robbo. Robbo swiftly kicked it to 'Smashing Sols', who then gave it an almighty boot. It was a powerful, good-looking torpedo kick. The ball shot high into the sky, arcing its way down towards Specky.

The torpedo punt, when kicked properly, covers more ground than any other kick. It travels in a spiral motion through the air, and requires a lot of practice. The ball is held at an angle, across your body, and should make contact with the middle to outside part of your foot. There is a big margin for error and

a lot of torpedoes go horribly wrong and drop short or fly off the side of the boot. But the one that spins correctly is a work of art and a delight to watch.

This was his big chance to impress Bob, so Specky hoped he was watching, as he took to the air at the same time as three other opponents who were going up for a mark. Specky was wedged in among the others. The pack flew, and all four boys had their hands only centimetres away from the ball.

Suddenly, one of the players accidentally swung back his elbow, right in between Specky's eyes. It was a painful blow, and Specky dropped to the ground with a gut-wrenching thud. The umpire blew his whistle to halt the game.

'Oh, no! Speck!' shouted Danny and Robbo, who could see it was a pretty hard knock.

Specky was out cold. He lay motionless on the moist grass.

Coach Pappas and the other supporters rushed out to Specky's side. Bob was nowhere to be seen.

'Give us some space! Stand back!' yelled Coach Pappas, as he knelt down beside Specky.

'Specky? Speck? Can you hear me?'

There was no response. The coach checked Specky's pulse — he was still breathing, but only just. 'C'mon, lad. Wake up!' he said, tapping him gently on the face.

But still no response. Everyone looked on in horror. This was a serious injury.

'Call an ambulance!' shouted a concerned voice, bursting through the crowd.

'Who are you?' asked the umpire.

'I'm the boy's father.'

Danny and Robbo couldn't believe their eyes as they looked up to see that it was indeed Specky's dad, Mr Magee. Bob was still nowhere to be seen.

'Yes, he's right. Call for some help!' added Coach Pappas. 'He could have a spinal or neck injury, so don't move him!'

It was only minutes before the howling siren came screeching to the scene. The ambulance officers bolted across the oval to Specky, and after checking him out, gently placed him onto a stretcher and loaded him in the back of the ambulance. Mr Magee jumped into the back with Specky, and they sped off to the hospital.

7 HOURS LATER ...

Specky was still unconscious in his hospital bed. The doctor had put an oxygen mask on him, and attached all sorts of wires to his body and head. The hospital staff and Specky's family waited anxiously, hoping and praying he would wake up. Throughout the day, Coach Pappas, Danny, Robbo, Specky's team-mates, and even Christina and her dad had tried to visit but were prevented from doing so by the doctors — only family members were allowed by Specky's bedside. Instead they left their good wishes at reception.

'Oh my God!' whispered Alice. Specky was opening one of his eyelids.

'Hey, squirt. Can you hear me?'

Specky groaned.

'Oh my God! He's waking up!' she screamed. Alice jumped up out of her seat and pressed the buzzer by Specky's bed to notify the doctor and nurses.

'Alice?' mumbled Specky. Both of his eyes were now open.

'Yeah, it's me. You just keep still and don't panic. I'm going to get Mum and Dad!'

Specky was confused. He grabbed Alice's arm before she had a chance to leave. 'Where am I?' he gasped, under the oxygen mask.

'You're in hospital. You were knocked out at footy today, remember?'

'Where's Bob? Did he see me mark?'

'Bob? Who cares about him! He did a runner, Si. He didn't even see you get hit. He left a message on the answering machine saying he had to head back up to Sydney. He had some stupid audition. He doesn't even know you're here. Dad helped the ambulance guys take you off the oval.'

Specky removed the oxygen mask and coughed a couple of times. 'Dad? What was he doing at the game?' he said.

'He was watching you from a distance, in his car. He didn't want you or Bob to see him.'

Just then the doctor and two nurses rushed in. Alice ran off to get her parents, who were having a break in the hospital canteen.

'How many fingers can you see?' asked the doctor, holding up his hand.

'Four,' answered Specky correctly.

'What's your phone number?'

Specky correctly recited his home number.

'Simon!' cried Specky's mother, dashing into the room. She hugged him tightly.

'Well, initial signs look good. But we'll have to keep him in for two or three days observation.

We'll also schedule him in for a brain scan,' said the doctor to Specky's dad.

'Dad,' muttered Specky.

Specky's mother and the doctor stood aside, to let Specky's father get in closer.

Specky stared up at his dad for a moment, and tears started to well up in his eyes. His father leaned down and hugged him.

'It's all right. I'm here,' he whispered into Specky's ear.

'I'm sorry, Dad. I'm sorry ... '

'Hey, shhh, it's okay. *I'm* the one who should be sorry.'

Specky knew at that very moment that there was no other father for him than the man who was holding him right there and then. He may not have been a 'footy dad', but he was a father who was there for him when it really mattered — and that's the best sort of dad anyone could ever ask for.

'I love you,' mumbled Specky.

'I love you too, son.'

Two weeks later ...
Specky and his team-mates stumbled off the footy oval. They were happy with another victory. With less than half a season to go, they

felt confident about their winning streak. They all looked forward to the coming weeks, the finals, and the adventures that were sure to come from them.

'Great game, Simon. You are *so* good! I had no idea you were such a talent,' gushed Specky's dad, beaming proudly. He had watched the entire match.

'Before you go and get changed, there's something I want to ask you,' he said, ruffling Specky's hair.

'What?' asked Specky.

Specky's father pulled something out of his bag — a brand new football.

'I was wondering if you could teach your old man how to kick one of these things?'

Specky's entire face lit up. He had the biggest grin that any 12-year-old boy who loved footy could ever have.

'You bet!'

Felice Arena grew up in the small Victorian town of Kyabram. He then went on to study at La Trobe University in Bendigo, Victoria. He graduated as a primary school teacher, but decided instead to pursue his love for acting and writing.

As an actor he played Marco Alessi in 'Neighbours' for a year; starred on the London West End stage in the musicals *Hair*, *Godspell*, *Joseph*, and *What a Feeling*; guest appeared on many television dramas; presented children's TV (Saturday Disney UK); and performed in numerous pantomimes and commercials.

As a writer Felice's books are published by HarperCollins Publishers in Australia, Britain and Canada. They are *Dolphin Boy Blue* (shortlisted for the Lancashire Book Award, UK), *Mission Buffalo*, *Wish* (shortlisted for the Western Australia Young Readers Award 2000/2001), *Bravo, Billy!*, *Breakaway John*, and of course, *Specky Magee*.

For further information about Felice and his books, visit his website at:

www.felicearena.com

Garry Lyon was one of the stars of the AFL throughout the late eighties and nineties.

Recruited from Kyabram, Garry made an immediate impression at the Melbourne Football Club. Able to play key positions at both ends of the ground he made state selection in 1988 and was a regular after that.

Garry was an outstanding player. He won club Best and Fairest twice, gained All-Australian selection and led the club's goal-kicking. His on-field presence and outstanding play made him an ideal captain, a post he held from 1991 to 1997.

In the last few years of his career Garry was dogged by a serious back injury, his fearless style of play contributing to his run of injuries. Eventually, the injuries caught up with him and in 1999 Garry announced his retirement, ending a remarkable career.

Garry now appears on Channel 9, Nova 100, the DMG radio group and writes for *The Herald Sun*.

MORE GREAT YOUNGER READER
BOOKS FROM HARPERCOLLINS

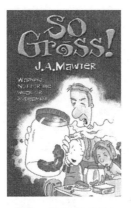

SO GROSS!

J. A. MAWTER

Chewed spew flew across the room, covering everything in its path. You couldn't tell who was who. Undigested eyeballs stared up at them. Piles of puke landed on the floor and great gobs of goo splotched onto the table. It looked like there'd been an almighty food fight.

What do chewed spew, blue smoke farts, a boogie collection and black poo have in common? They're all *So Gross!* A hilarious collection of seven of the funniest and most revolting stories ever, *So Gross!* is for lovers of the fouler things in life. This repulsive collection of demented stories is definitely not for the squeamish, and should not, under any circumstances, be read on a full stomach.

ISBN 0 207 19733 4

PIGGOTT PLACE

DUNCAN BALL

Piggott Place is a riotous but touching comedy about twelve-year-old Bert Piggott as he struggles to keep his family of dreamers, ratbags and scoundrels together. Everyone hates the Piggotts and now the council is going to evict them from their once beautiful mansion, Piggott Place. But the authorities haven't bargained on Bert and his young friend Antigone (would-be star of stage and screen) and their crazy scheme. The question is: can two kids take on a world of adults and win?

'A humorous, well-written novel with numerous twists and turns which devotees of Ball's Selby books should thoroughly enjoy.'

READING TIME

ISBN 0 207 19979 5

PIGGOTTS IN PERIL

DUNCAN BALL

Piggotts in Peril begins with the shy and sensitive Bert Piggott accidentally finding the map to pirate treasure hidden many years ago by his great-great-great-great-grandfather. At first a quest for untold wealth seems the answer to all his problems but getting it means bringing along his scheming, ratbag family. Little does he know that what lies ahead are problems that even the pessimistic Bert could never imagine: the terror of turbulent seas aboard a 'borrowed' boat, capture by pirates, being marooned on the Isle of the Dead, and more.

Piggotts in Peril is a warm, adventure-comedy about the origins of the universe, the evolution of humankind — and pirate treasure.

ISBN 0 207 19783 0

I AM JACK

SUSANNE GERVAY

Jack likes going to school. He enjoys learning
George Hamel calls Jack — Bum Head.
All the kids at school call Jack — Bum Head.
Jack's in BIG trouble ... school is getting dangerous.
Nobody seems to want to listen. Until one day...

'*I Am Jack* celebrates kids. Unique, valuable kids. Bullying isolates and victimises children. *I Am Jack* shows them that they are not alone and can win against bullying.'

LIFE EDUCATION AUSTRALIA

ISBN 0 207 19905 1

EMILY EYEFINGER
AND THE DEVIL BONES
DUNCAN BALL

Emily Eyefinger's parents were shocked when Emily was born with an eye on the end of her finger BUT ... Emily has discovered that an eye on the end of her finger can be very handy!

In the title story of this exciting new collection of Emily Eyefinger's adventures, Emily finds the bones of an ancient, extinct mouse. This mammoth mouse was as big an elephant and terrified the cats of its day. But no sooner does Emily make her discovery than the so-called 'Devil Bones' go missing. Once again, Emily searches for a solution to an ever-deepening mystery.

ISBN 0 207 19775 X

SELBY'S SELECTION
DUNCAN BALL

Here's the collection you have been waiting for — a super selection of the silliest, side-splitting stories chosen by Selby himself. Plus there are stacks of new jokes, poems, songs and other saucy surprises from the only talking dog in Australia and, perhaps, the world.

Selby is the mutt with the mostest, the punch-packing pooch, the dashing daring dog from Down Under. And he's hanging out to have big, big fun! So strap yourselves in, hold onto your sides and get ready for the very best of Selby.

ISBN 0 20719772 5